Anansi

Taken

ALSO BY DAPHNE MARLATT

Taken

Daphne Marlatt

Published in 1996 by
House of Anansi Press Limited
1800 Steeles Avenue West, Concord, ON
Canada   L4K 2P3

Distributed in Canada by
General Distribution Services Inc.
30 Lesmill Road
Toronto, Canada   M3B 2T6
Tel. (416) 445-3333
Fax (416) 445-5967
e-mail: Customer.Service@ccmailgw.genpub.com

Distributed in the United States by
General Distribution Services Inc.
85 River Rock Drive, Suite 202
Buffalo, New York 14207
Toll free 1-800-805-1083
Fax (416) 445-5967
e-mail: Customer.Service@ccmailgw.genpub.com

CATALOGING IN PUBLICATION DATA

Marlatt, Daphne, 1942–
Taken

ISBN 0-88784-587-8

I. Title.

PS8576.A74T34 1996   C813'.54   96-990096-1
PR9199.3.M36T34 1996

Cover design: Bill Douglas @ The Bang
Printed and bound in Canada
Typesetting: ECW Type & Art

*House of Anansi Press gratefully acknowledges the support of the Canada Council
and the Ontario Arts Council in the development of writing and publishing in Canada.*

In memory of my mother and father

My loves are dying. Or is it that my love
is dying, day by day, brief life, brief candle,
a flame, *flambeau*, torch, alive, singing
somewhere in the shadow: Here, this way, here.

— Phyllis Webb, *Water and Light*

I

⌐ GHOST LEAVES come up in the half-light, translating themselves from misty grey to yellow, that bright, luminous yellow of
November still hanging on, tentative, as if about to fade away at
the slightest provocation. And she begins to coalesce somewhere
behind my eyes, behind the hand over my mouth (my mouth, as
if i should not say anything, not yet, not now), staring at space
through which those leaves glimmer, alder and fern in the wet
earth . . .

There were ferns where she was in the Blue Mountains of
Australia, tree ferns the height of her hip. That was Leura, that
was Katoomba, that was staving off despair, praying, willing
him to safety, no, pleading, pleading with God, with Destiny,
that he would return. War time, black and white time, whole
cultures reduced to dirty adjectives under the acrid developer
of national will. What was one individual, one tiny life in all of
that?

⌐

Will was something Esme always had trouble with. Will, backbone, being brave, whatever words they used. All the way back to that private hell of field hockey games at school. She doesn't think about England, she puts England, which is suffering air raids and rationing, out of her mind. There are strident bird calls from the gardens outside, there is the sound of teatime conversation from the terrace. She doesn't want to go down and listen yet again to émigré English matrons bewailing their relatives' deprivation. Behind the façade of routine civility, so well-maintained, she feels his absence opening like a void she has failed to prepare for. They are travellers trapped in transit by the Japanese invasion of Malaya. Well, she is — he has gone off headlong to meet the crisis, and time, that carpet that once unrolled before them, lush with carefully figured plans, has been pulled out from under by some much larger hand.

She curls up in a corner of the sofa in her room gazing at the black and white photo on the table beside her. It is one of the few images of herself she actually likes.

There they are, together on a Melbourne street, her hand laced through his arm, her breast just under his elbow. The forward motion of their step stilled for a second by some street photographer she is smiling for, having just caught the camera's swivel toward them. Smiling at the lens, a slight distance under her half-closed lids, mouth smiling as she says, "Darling, he's snapping us." Yes, she is pretty, yes, she is with a man who adores her, yes, they are at the turning point of history in this part of the world, though she hadn't known it then. She'd been too thrilled by the turn in their own private history.

He is looking askance, frowning slightly at something he doesn't approve of, or something that worries him, more probably, because he is leaning slightly toward her under his rather

4

high-crowned fedora placed straight on his head. He's carrying her shopping bag and managing to look both proper in sports jacket and tie, and casual in baggy flannels. How she loves the boyishness of that combination, his grin which is not in the picture but which she could have provoked in the following instant. What was he looking at? A newsboy, she thinks now, a headline. Already preoccupied with war, the signs of destiny running ahead of their moment.

But she, she was only there in that moment given back to her, the surprise and pleasure of a stranger's snapping them on that day, in that split second. Because she's feeling confident for once, redeemed. The kickpleat of her frock billows out before her under the coat she's holding, bag tucked under her arm, hat-brim slanted pertly over one eye — a small-brimmed sombrero under a cloud of white net framing her soft hair. White hat, white shoes, white bag and then the light-coloured dress, tailored. Perfect against his darker attire, his conscientious face with its long, regal-looking nose (King George, she thinks), his astute eye.

But there like an omen behind them strides an Australian officer in army khaki, heel down, sole up marching step. Even in his naval uniform, Charles would never look like that, self-satisfied. And there, too, under the awning of the shop they were walking by, a woman in a dress of thin stripes (might have been slimming, but the bodice runs one way, skirt the other) has paused, one foot on the step, head tipped toward the window and its invisible goods. Probably thinking about money, balancing whatever has caught her eye with whatever is in her cheque-book. The black seam of her stocking runs straight down to her high-heeled and very black shoe, the shoe too heavy really for that light dress, especially on a spring day. (Heaviness everywhere — how to avoid fear. . . ?)

5.

That was an October morning, Flinders Lane. Late spring with the surprising warmth of summer (she hasn't got used to being back in the seasons again). That was the morning the Collins Street specialist told her she was pregnant. They were on their way out to lunch to celebrate. And if they hadn't been on leave in Australia to visit her parents, on holiday, really, when Malaya was invaded — ? She doesn't like to think about it. And now, after their stroke of luck, Charles *would* decide he had to go back — to do his duty he said. What could she say against duty?

—

Faint leaves come up in the half-light — leafings out and leavings, these passages — and i can almost touch her skin, the softness of it with that faint brown down. Mingy, she said, complaining about her eyelashes that had fallen out when she applied some patent thickener to them — how old was she then? All her life complaining about her hair that would not keep a perm. Yet — I like Chinese men, she said, they don't have all that disgusting body hair.

Body compulsions. Skin on skin. And the story that was handed down included her fantasy of Chinese blood somewhere in the family, or was it Indian? and was it a fantasy? Her mother's scandalized denial. Only later did i find out what people thought of them in Penang — "chi chi," they said when my father proposed to her, mixed blood.

There was the story and there was the real presence of her body which i knew elementally, apart from its history. Only now do i search out the traces, eager to know what shaped her, how she became who she was, Esme, the woman of a photographed reality i never knew. The world they lived in then.

—

6

Beach parties off Batu Ferringhi, jaunts up Penang Hill to the Crag Hotel with its stupendous sunsets, bats soaring over their heads, drives out to the freshwater pools at Titi Krawang in Freddy the Fiat, excursions to Muka Head. Names with the resonance of nostalgia throbbing in them, tiny arteries to a past that was once living. And what is nostalgia but the longing for place the body opens to, the very taste of it on one's skin. Ah, but the Straits Settlements, about as far as one could get from England — or from Canada — as exotic a home as one could adopt, if never, never belong in, was still a colony on the fringe of the mother country's skirts.

England was no mother to Esme, born in India, though she, like her parents, continually referred to it as "home." Home that was not, misplaced home that could never be. Where did one belong?

Ghosts are those who occupy a place, but not in the flesh, those who are left with only the memory-trace of it on their tongues.

—

Night, the depth of not-seeing before light begins to silhouette shapes we can identify. At night we could be anywhere. In the dark i startle from unremembered dream, losing indolent edges, my body's warm uncurling float in tropical seas. I listen, stiff, for clues.

This is island yes, but temperate island. Cedar and fir murmur between houses of brief acreage along the lakeshore, and then, only a little way over on either side, straits between our island and the next. Clouds lie low, muffling the lake so one can't hear its shifting in the night. Eagles and ravens are elsewhere, sleep-ruffled. Only owls hunt on deadly wings, and the raccoons, just

7

as menacing to cats, head through the trees for our compost heap.

Still in the nest we have made of our bodies in bed, burrowed into each other, i inhale the odour of your skin, deeply familiar. I want to sink beyond place, lost, in the "o" my lips make around the smooth berry of your nipple. When suddenly a voice comes through the trees, boiling its words into something i can't quite make out — "RICH-ard! RICH-ard!" is it? two-toned, cracked.

Still curled, my face on your shoulder, i hear your breathing break to alarmed listening. Who is she calling? Richard i think. We listen. It doesn't sound like Nell. Who else would it be? The voice stops, then boils up and over.

She's in some kind of despair, i say. It's rage, you say. We lie awake, images of what could trigger such emotion flickering through our heads.

What if she needs help? You sigh and turn over. Sure. I can just see us — the dykes next door turned marriage counsellors.

So trees, yes, trees and a property line. But scarcely woods and hardly deep enough to stop these odd lines of connection ringing through the night.

—

Did she find the nights quiet in Leura? Up in the mountains, blue with the sighing of a million gum trees, that aromatic breath in the night reminding her of colds, her father's salve and the flannel cloths her mother heated for her once in their brief stay in London. Fog and coal dust, how they hated it. The poor relations, the small, smutty backyard.

8

She wanted orchids, armloads of orchids. She wanted colour and tropical explosions of smell, running water over hot pavement, the rake of Kabun's twig broom in the grass, always, everywhere, the melodic hubbub of voices in unknown languages, bullock hooves, bicycle tires, a tiny orchestra of frogs deafening the night. Not war, not this incessant talk of airfields and tanks and battalions fighting their way through jungle.

The Japanese took Penang, then Kuala Lumpur, and advanced on Malacca. Charles cabled her from Java, "Not Proceeding to Singapore." What did it mean? After days of anxious waiting, a letter arrived from a hotel in Batavia, informing her that he had joined the Royal Navy as Paymaster Sub-Lieutenant.

In January 1942, writing to celebrate his birthday, "the only form of celebration that will take place," he tells her. "You will realize that I am very comfortably placed, living in a hotel. The only snag is that the hours of work are such that there is never any spare time. We work in watches, as on board ship i.e. 4 hour & 2 hour periods at all times of the day & night . . . We get only one proper night's sleep every 3 days. Our spare time is thus devoted to eating, bathing, dealing with the dhoby, trying to order uniform & sleeping at all sorts of odd hours. There has not even been time to sit down quietly & enjoy a stengah . . ."

—

Stengah — the word explodes with its flash of associations. Not just the actual taste of whiskey and soda, the blue siphon bottle with its silver handle, not just the Chinese liquor cabinet in the corner of the lounge across from double doors opening onto the terrace, his legs crossed in their white ducks on the low settee, a cigarette from the vacuum-sealed pewter cannister trailing its scent through the room in the wake of office stories and her news of tiffin at the Runnymede with Dorothy and Molly, or a shopping foray into the cloth bazaar. Stengahs at the Club, shimmer of evening dress and jewellery. Stengahs on outdoor tables at the Lone Pine Hotel as the sun flamed down behind the casuarina trees and the blood-warm sea rolled in. Though ayer limaus — water and lime — was what she usually ordered, "or else," her light laugh, self-deprecating, "I'm afraid I'd be under the table." The feel of salt on her skin, hair still wet, the chatter of friends, small lamps swinging overhead as the dark blanketed their shoulders suddenly ruffling them with the promise of cool. It was their stage pre-war, "the real Malaya," as the British would always think.

But she hadn't liked swimming — at least in the aftermath. She preferred to sit in the sand in what i always saw as her elegant costume, heart-shaped neck, low enough for the rise of her breasts to show, straps crossed over wingbones at back, the woollen bathing costumes everyone wore that would have taken hours to dry on an English beach but didn't in the hot wind coming off the Straits of Malacca. Fingers in dank wet sand, deftly cutting pieces of rambutan, slicing them open neatly through their greenish hair. Liquid sections of mangosteen, so difficult to pry from their tough brown shell with its scarlet inside staining our fingers and everything we touched.

Hawkers going by in their sarongs, or calling to us from roadside wheeled stands. Kerosene lamps, sizzling palm oil, the strong smell of fuel from the motor that pressed out sugarcane juice. Urgent talk, calls we didn't understand, mangy pi-dogs, mouthwatering smells of food we weren't allowed to buy. And that sense of danger as night fell and we were still out in it, not safely barricaded under yards of mosquito netting behind iron grillework and the doors that had never been locked pre-war, locked now.

—

Or perhaps she was not really there at all but longing to be with him, imagining herself there in his hotel room sharing his snatched hours of sleep (poor darling). Imagining his day off when they would explore the city, Javanese temple dancers (said to be beautiful), Javanese batik (the most gorgeous sarongs) . . . Tourists in wartime. No, she knew it was absurd. She had to remember Singapore, she had to remember that she was pregnant and could only be a liability. Besides, there were her parents. Her duty, as her mother would remind her, was to stay here with them and cheer him on from the sidelines. But the idea of turning up to surprise him, hiding in his room with a platter of fruit, a stengah or two for his weary self . . . Her imagining went that far, as far as herself in cheong sam . . . hibiscus in her hair, hair not her own, baby-fine pale brown, but hair that swung as she moved, thick and glistening like some concubine's . . . Isn't that what he would like? Isn't that what all men liked? And why did women have to advertise their availability by wearing that showy flower? Its vulgar centre so nude, so terrifying . . .

Like a pang it struck: if only she could have given herself — that phrase, _given_ herself — just once, just once holding nothing back. Why did she always feel instead it was being taken from her? Despite his patience, his tenderness. He wasn't like other men, he loved her in such a different way. It might not be too late, please God, it couldn't be. She would reopen her younger conversations with Him. She would call on Him daily, hourly if need be.

"I thanked God on reading your letter that you were not to go to Singapore. It was dreadful reading about all the raids in the paper — & wondering if you might have gone on after all — but I felt you would not have cabled me if it were not pretty definite . . . I can't help feeling that it is more than mere coincidence how things have planned out — & I have prayed so hard for your good — & for your safety that I feel God surely must hear my prayers."

To be taken, if necessary, with him. That was the thought that interrupted her praying. Not to be left. Alone. (Though she would not be, with the baby, but the baby seemed unreal, a possibility not to be borne — its presence and his loss.) "Awake, my Little ones, and fill the Cup / Before Life's Liquor in its Cup be Dry." They had sipped at such a Cup together, but sipped only. Always there was the intervening taste of something metallic as silver paper, something like fear. Of what? Something she could not put her finger on. It shadowed her in some other dimension, a curse, a destiny the Ouija glass had tapped out once, in front of them all. Death insane in a foreign country.

Darling, don't take it so seriously, her mother had purred, nothing like that could possibly happen to you. What did she know beyond the social niceties? She who could warmly greet somebody's wife at a hospital bazaar and then rip her appearance to shreds in the car on the way home.

No, whatever it was had brought her gentle Charles, twelve years older and so eligible he could have had any girl in the colony, might yet veer, reverse direction. And she, relying on what she was not even sure she had, that mixture of prettiness and wit, and some strange clarity that drove her to defiance at times, could yet do nothing against it. And so she called on

12

God. And reminded herself that it was Charles who was in peril, Charles she would strike a bargain for. Writing against his absence, against fate to bring him close.

"Darling — I am sure you must look very handsome in your naval uniform — do please send me a snap of yourself by air-mail as soon as you can. I hate to think of you being so poor that you have to ride on trams instead of a taxi — & share a room in a cheap Hotel — while I live in comfort here — but as you say we have to be so thankful that you are not sleeping on the benches or in camp in S.

"I do hope you will not have to go to sea!!!"

—

What benches? I only see the bombed-out church, where in the gloom beggars slept on what was left of pews, or on cement, half-dead, mute. Or muttering in the street, pointing to their stumps or sightless eyes. Beggars with blown-off limbs, beggars with burnt hands held out like small cages closing in.

That's St. George's, she used to say, where your father and I were married. Such a beautiful church, who could imagine it would end up a ruin? At night, lifting the veils of mosquito netting to find me in my terror, she wondered why i dreamed about beggars. They can't hurt you, poor things. (And what about bombs?)

And how did she soothe herself before i knew her?

Sitting with her copy of Khayyám, the one her father had given her, having inscribed it for her birthday in his declarative hand (the shadow of his intentions for her present in his choice of words), "The Moment Opportune":

One Moment in Annihilation's Waste,
One Moment, of the Well of Life to taste —

Believing in God still, and the efficacy of prayer. Believing in The Potter and the strength of his Pots. Not a mis-made, not a mislaid one, certainly none brushed with a sparrow's wing-feather. Did this extend to a Tamil beggar?

Then, back then, the beggars were only slightly more gaunt than the rickshaw wallahs. She saw them halt panting between the poles, ribs straining out from under skin, as their well-fed passengers descended, fanning themselves. What of the lives of the rickshaw wallahs?

Nonsense, her father said when she had first come out from boarding school, full of Shelley and Tennyson. They at least can earn their bowl of rice. They're fortunate men compared to the beggars.

She supposed the girls at St. Nicholas' School for the Blind were fortunate then: their fingers earned their keep by feel, smocking brightly coloured threads in dresses for European missees. Charles, who acted as treasurer for the school, had taken her to see them. That was one of the reasons her father had approved of him: his interest in the blind.

Poor things, her mother sighed after their visit to the school when Charles stayed on for dinner — but darling, I do hope you didn't touch any of them. For God's sake, Aylene, Viktor waved away the tureen of brinjal slices the Boy was offering (the Boy who never remembered that he disliked them, or did and was being deliberately stupid), how many times must I tell you, it isn't syphilis.

Such table manners, darling! Aylene laughed sharply and glanced at Esme who seemed distressed by the dog. Curled up

14

by the table, he had begun to clean his privates with considerable relish. In Charles' presence even Paddy was failing them.

Now Esme reflected that her mother must have taken satisfaction in the appalling innocence of her blush. It would have proven her belief in the charms of innocence. Later, in response to her embarrassed query on the night before the wedding, the only advice had been, Let Charles show you, my dear. After all, most girls were immoral, Aylene maintained, a hazard of life in the colonies, and it was this that made them unappealing to the better sort of men.

———

Otters live here with all the pleasure of beings who belong. Three of them diving for clams like butter sliding into water, their dark coats slicked back. Just as the dark space behind the trees begins to brighten, they appear on the dock, slithering along its frosted planks to scratch their backs, delicate paws waving in sheer pleasure.

Knotting and unknotting ourselves by candlelight, i think of them even as we submerge in hunger searching out the soft parts, undoing nipples, lips with tongue talk, parading it, for that long final shout. Then gone in our own foetal curl, soft gone and long gone, impossible to know where each of us ends.

How put it together with the news we are occupied by, preoccupied, so that this fades. As the war machine gears up across all media, "There's no way around it," diagrams enter the paper, Tomahawk cruise missile, Apache helicopter, TOW anti-tank missile, "the deadliest threat," — good old boys waging their epithets, their death-curse. Once it begins, where does it end?

Enclosed here — as if becalmed. The days slide by in a slow gel woods and water suspend. Nothing we do has any consequence. The fatal idea of islands cut off from the main.

———

Had she written "beaches" and i simply read "n" for "a"? Sleeping on the beaches an image of dereliction, image of an army in rout. Abandoned in either case. Despite mosquito netting and the coolest of cotton sheets, or later, in Melbourne, the warmest of blankets, all requisite, her sleep frayed at the edges, unravelled at the slightest sound. Trying to touch his new life in Batavia, she yet wishes for him all the creature comforts they shared as Tuan and Mem. While he meets her touch with his own, writing to recoup their membership in a world that is shattering around them:

"I have met two people from Penang on the street here. One was your old pal Manuelo the Hairdresser. He had been sent out of Malaya on medical grounds & was in such a hurry to see the Free French Consul that there was no time to talk. The other was Mrs. Durham who has got a job here on the army staff. Mrs. D. was also in a hurry as she was expecting to be transferred somewhere the next day, but I did obtain the following news from her:

(a) The women & children in Penang were not evacuated on December the 9th. They had a week's bombardment before they left.

(b) Peggy went down to Singapore with the rest of them & had her baby in Singapore."

Such news! And all the same she scans his letter anxiously for love, the familiar endearments, some sign that he has not

16

become a stranger. Convinced that if not now then
tears prick — and just when their child is on its way
she thinks, stop thinking. Tears of rage at her own weakness.

Hearing that Fifth Form hockey voice she loathed, Chin up,
girls, she laces on her walking shoes. Find a place, somewhere
in that ferny growth under the gumtrees leaning cinematic over
descending views, where she can stand alone . . . The place
where they had promised to think of each other at this time of
day, just when the light begins to blue, but does he, can he?
Pause for a second in the middle of a watch to see her in Leura
at the edge of the bush imagining, trying so hard to imagine
him there? He knows the Blue Mountains, he can see her in her
pleated skirt (soon to be unwearable), short-sleeved blouse (her
fuller breasts are making it gape a little), standing just where
they had admired the view. But the clogged streets of Batavia,
his regimented life, are sealed away from her. She tries to
imagine a feverish activity, refugees mingling with the military
on streets that now, with the siege of Singapore, have become
headquarters for the Far East war effort. "We see all the big shots
here," he wrote cheerfully, careful not to name them, knowing
the censor's eye was scanning every word of the neatly inked
lines he wrote, even no doubt his faintly pencilled "notes
overleaf."

As for the streets of Singapore, where Peggy will not be alone,
but under terrifying conditions, and with a newborn. So Peggy's
had her baby — boy or girl? he doesn't say, perhaps Mrs.
Durham didn't know. Did they get away by ship or did she have
to travel all the way down the peninsula by train? Imagine, that
far along and having to travel under bombs. The baby must have
been premature. How could one bear the rattling and jostling
of a train, the fear of surprise attack at any moment, a blown up

17

bridge perhaps, or worse, possible capture? And what about Penang? what remains of it now?

She is trying to confront something as she stands in the blue dusk blurring air around her — the scale of this disaster in their lives. Not just her dresses, her china, her beautiful rooms. Not just her servants — hiding, she hopes, up in the hills. Company estates gone, lives in ruin, friends scattered. Jack was with the Volunteers, fighting in the jungle somewhere. Did Peggy even know where? And what about the hospital and her father's cronies? Medical staff wouldn't flee, would they? But what would life be like under Japanese occupation?

Looking at the larger picture helps to ease the void of Charles' goodbye (don't come to the dock, don't come to Sydney, he said, it will only make things that much harder). But the larger picture, go back to that, how they are all in it together. How the tiny being growing deep inside her doesn't know despair, goes on growing, pushing out her waist, happily oblivious inside her flesh.

Perspective, she rages, as her tears dry clean in the aromatic wind.

And if Singapore falls, then what about Java . . . ? She will not think it (she is twenty-three and knows how to close certain doors). He will be safe in Batavia. She wills it, she puts herself in league with God, God willing or D.V. as her mother always adds, a charm against catastrophe. She turns on her heel in her brown walking shoe, crushing her hanky into a small ball. You must occupy yourself — her mother again, sententious with the security of having an ailing husband to care for. She will, she will write letters, pray, eat, sleep, grow a baby as if nothing could possibly happen . . . D.V.

18

Driving you to the ferry, along the upper road in early morning dark, its sudden turns flanked by darker walls of fir and cedar, you sit wrapped in thought in the blue glow of the dash and the white beam of our forward going. Until our lights pick out two deer, a fawn and a doe who stare across the road at a smaller movement disappearing . . . What was it? Transfixed they stand, reading, perhaps, the tail end of a cat. And then, as we roar by, they're gone.

What do cat and deer make of each other? And then this apocalyptic machine splitting their world for an instant. Even as dark closes in beyond us, tree walls of dark enfolding a world cats and other creatures inhabit.

Not the kind of thing to muse about to somebody on the brink of a journey, especially a journey to the States.

On the other (the same?) side of our world bombers have exploded the Baghdad night. Operation Desert Storm is underway and our papers are alive with threats of terrorism. A new vocabulary has taken hold: Tomahawk cruise missiles and Stealth fighters, plague-laden warheads, a holy war.

Faced with this chasm, this sense of an enemy again, we sit in half-light, holding hands around the gearshift. A random cluster of foot passengers stands by the empty ticket booth, gazing off into dawn air.

Beyond the terminal, your ferry hums white and huge, galley crew busy with breakfast, lights broadcast on dark water. You wait til the last minute because, with all our putting down roots on this island, it still isn't easy when one of us leaves — especially now. I think of the mandrake and the tiny shriek it is supposed to give when it is pulled.

You'll remember the hydro bill? Of course. (You think i'm hopelessly disorganized . . .) And you'll get the tree man to check out that fir? We don't want it coming down on our heads. I know, i know (. . . lured back into island time, its lack of imperatives. A luxury we can no longer afford).

—

Writing her desire against the destiny script, tense with the meshes of circumstance, she pens a P.S., trying to sound off-hand: "I met a Dutch woman today whose husband is in Java — & she said as far as she knew women could return to Java — if I were not going to have a baby I could have joined you darling — a bit tough isn't it? I had better stay til after Aug. any way — I suppose. What do you think dearest?"

He doesn't say. Or at least there is no letter answering this. A query that if followed up would have put her in one of the internment camps, an official term for slow dying. But those dashes in her question, the lingering "I suppose," suggest hesitation, the pressure perhaps of her father's voice — Use your head, my girl! You'd be nothing but a millstone round his neck. And something else — not wanting to risk it? not feeling she could muster the requisite heroism?

In any case, a different hope expresses itself further on: "perhaps there might be a chance of your being transferred to Sydney or Melbourne — I know it is asking too much but still — there just might be a slender chance — wouldn't it be grand?"

She knows she is writing against his manly duty, his heroism, her role as dutiful wife. Planting the thought in his mind, using their familiar language, appealing to the lover in him. Come back.

20

As the branches assume dim shapes in the half-light, there, really there outside in the dark, my connection fades. I don't know what else to call it — this limitless space that awakens me early in the morning when i open to her presence in a way i never could when she was alive — or only in the very beginning perhaps. Mother and child. That nameless interbeing we began with. Anxiety pushes me out of bed in the dark, to write her, reach her, bring her bodily out of the nothing, which is not nothing because she is there, leaning against me on the other side of a thin membrane that separates, so thin we communicate, but not in words. I reach toward her with these half-truths, half-light fading into ordinary time and space.

No, she is somewhere else, she always was.

But here, here is the cat i stroke. He jumps up, rubbing against paper, insisting his presence. Stroke — a word that fails to convey the rhythm fingers make in fur, responding to his torso writhing under my hand. He purrs, tail lashes, almost giving in, almost thinking to escape, still wiry with the large and barely perceptible waking of the world outdoors — he has only just come in, paws still fragrant with earth.

Do words keep us branching here rather than there where the dreams are? wordless in another landscape, other bodies' lives, bodies that skim the air above foreign gardens, bodies that swim under water, breathing there. And i come surfacing into my own, with only the faintest memory, intact in my skin, these words that want to register being here. As if now, in the long moment before dawn, i sense what it is not to be.

Oh Lori, i suppose i could send this as a letter to you there in Iowa, you with your mother alive and needy, you in another

21

"here." (And would this image of our cat be a familiar wrench? Or would it seem a claim on you, strange, uncalled for?) Words, the words we usually speak to each other, are not at all the ones we write in secret and alone. Perhaps we've forgotten how to tell the secret, hesitant ones, the ones that verge on the very rim of silence.

—

They were married in 1937, two years before war broke out in Europe. They were married in what would have been an English spring but in Penang was clear heat, well ahead of the rainy season with its monsoon downpours, its muddy overflowing streets and ravaged blossoms.

She was nineteen. A transient smile as she walked off the tennis court in her whites, twisting her racquet, the scarf with its diaphanous bow tying her hair away from her face — pretty, but with something wistful in her smile.

Who is that girl? he'd asked. Dr. Aloyan's daughter. Chief M.O., newly arrived in Penang — but his wife's Anglo-Indian lilt and the family name suggested something not quite British. Charles didn't care. He was thirty-one and so far there'd been no girl he'd really wanted, despite the dances, the swimming and sailing weekends, the dinner parties. Auburn, affable, courteous, he'd had no trouble finding girls who were eager to marry. There must be more to life, he thought when he found himself inventing engagements at the Club to avoid yet another party at the bachelors' mess he shared with two of his mates.

She was remote in a way that appealed to him. Pathos in her eyes, fragility in her slight frame. Charming, yes, yet he could see her assessing people and situations with a cool eye. He left his visiting card at her parents' and, once vetted, managed to take her out. He learned that she was certain life in the tropics, at least her parents' life, held nothing for her. Determined to stay in England when they went on leave, she was anxious to get some training, in dress design she thought. One of her school friends, a woman she admired, was studying medicine. She had looked into nursing but her father put his foot down — No daughter of mine. . . . Through a whirl of dance music and dinner engagements, her levity slightly sardonic — My father, you see, believes he is my *Pilot face to face* — Charles discovered that they shared a certain language. Was it the poetry? The metaphysics? Instead of the usual banter he had come to expect on such occasions, he found they were discussing Chinese astrology, the penance rites of Thaipusam, the strangeness of life in the Orient. On Bishop Street, he caught himself gazing at jewellers' trays, wondering if a slim band of gold would keep her in Penang.

Six months later they were married with all the ceremony of a first-class colonial wedding. Service at St. George's, reception on the grounds of the European and Oriental Hotel. On the lawn by the guns facing out to sea, canna lilies flared a ragged amber all around them as they posed for photographs. White peau de soie and tulle, white velvet leaves and pearl. Her veil a thin cascade, transparent even, over a coquettish excuse for a hat. She stood almost solitary, demure, while he in his shantung suit leaned toward her, dangerously happy. That night she learned what honeymoons were for.

—

It wasn't as if she hadn't known flirtation — her clothes, her smile with just the suggestion of heavy lids, her bottles of scent (always the delicacy of that word — never perfume, too heavy, she said). There was that preposterous (and where does that word come from? he must have used it teasingly) straw hat which sat forever in its box but which she refused to throw out because it was the only relic of their time "before the children." Their outing on the rocks along Great Ocean Road — the Twelve Apostles perhaps, or The Arch — when he first started taking cine films. Sea smashing up around her like frozen lace, she posed by a crevasse, Antarctic wind whipping her fashionably baggy shorts, demure white ankle socks, hand gripping the impossible picture hat. Black straw, with a crown so flat it was almost unwearable, nothing to detract from a gigantic brim asplash in magenta, green, sunburst raffia flowers. Tied under her chin, tipped at a rakish angle so it shadowed her face — only her mouth visible, its pout lifting the corners into a tentative smile. The hat! tip it back, back! he must have shouted as she struggled to comply, still trying to keep her look for the camera as buffets of polar wind kept pushing it down. And so the moment lived on in black and white: evidence that she had once worn it.

Impossible to jump that other crevasse, between my eyes watching the film, my hands remembering the feel of black straw stiff with disuse, and her body there on the bed, brown deathspots already making their way to the surface of her skin. Her already-foretold end made real in Canada. Too late to believe in. No, go back to her body warm and cool in the wind off those rocks, her slightly embarrassed stance, eager to see herself as he saw her. To see, for a change, beyond the uncertainty she was intimate with and by which she defined herself.

She never thought of herself as innocent, though she was. Not worldly, not guilty, not harming — but also not unharmed. When there are ghosts there is always hunger: for the life

24

unlived, the knot that draws desire back, something unresolved and ongoing.

But then, then she felt herself alive with something new in her. Though she was living at a moment when dying had begun, dying and the flight from home, or what, with children, would begin to seem like home — that "foreign clime" any of them could end up dying for. Identifying not so much with the place or its people as with a circle of friends transplanted, like them, floating tendrils through each others' lives in gossip, Residency balls, *The Straits Times*, curry tiffin at the Club . . .

He wrote from Java:

"The Leylands are staying in this hotel waiting for a ship to Australia. I have given them your address so you will be hearing from them in the near future. Mrs. L. is due to have a baby in May so you can imagine what a time she has had during the last two months, but she is very cheerful."

And so in the hotel in Leura she received news of yet another friend, expectant and racing on short time ahead of invasion, capture, POW camp. That net that supported them in their high-life, high-wire act, beginning to fray, break under the pressure of a new reality.

—

So much i don't know, all that preceded me. Who she was. Who he was. The tentative deciphering of what gets passed along in body tissue, without words. Not so much their history even, but the ambiance of their lives, what they took for granted, the smell, the feel of their time my own beginning intercepted. I'm reaching for another kind of story, a story of listening way back in the body. And is this memory? Or fiction?

How put together a narrative of brightly coloured bits turned, turning as if to focus, and the falling patterns then. Beautiful forms. Illusions of continuity, of completion, made by mirrors.

—

Gula melaka. Crumbly dark brown palm sugar that isn't sweet until the sweetness hits your mouth after the muskiness. Put that together with down-to-earth oats, the comfortable taste of English porridge, bland as congee, and never spiced as congee might be with onion or meat. Porridge accompanied by a sprinkling of white sugar, a pour of white milk, the breakfast of a Surrey farming family for generations — linked with my father and gula melaka. Impossibly, because i can't imagine him eating both, as i have (illicitly) with santan — every word an opening, a small internal explosion. Amah in the kitchen insisting with her throaty voice and radiant smile, a smile that outshone doubt or refutation, that this, this bowl held out to me is milk. It's the way she says it, san/tan, an affectionate rhyme, a challenge to take what i know isn't milk, at least not Nestle's powdered milk that comes in cans, but something so much tastier, coconut shavings wrung out with water, the water turned milky, fragrant, sweet.

Gula melaka and santan appeared in the dining room only on Sundays, with the sago pudding that concluded curry tiffin. Otherwise, except for an occasional supper of mah mee, it was English fare, or as close as one could get with tinned this and powdered that.

And yet something about him escaped the conservative mold of a Surrey farming family, as his own father had also escaped, the first to make a career in the army (Malta, India, gassed in the trenches of World War One). This something spoke into

26

the shady stillness of a snake-infested stream and mused about his sense of connection with Penang, a past life perhaps, a spice merchant trading by junk down the coast of the South China Sea.

The romance of the East speaking? The romance that seized him as soon as he arrived, young chartered accountant on his first job in the Straits Settlements of the thirties. And what was romance but colonial sentimentality? The soft glove on the ruling hand?

Or had he begun to think in ways he never would have if he had stayed in London with some tradition-bound firm? Was this the inkling of a different way of being — a challenge, perhaps, to all he'd been raised with? Or was he just another young man who left England with a broken heart and the desire to mend himself in some new place?

A convivial man with a good sense of humour and an interest in things metaphysical, he admired the Chinese towkays he dealt with for the same qualities. He liked his stories well-told, his liquor cabinet well-stocked, his accounts in exquisite order. Appreciation, in all things, was his profoundest principle.

—

Caught in the initial chaos of the Pacific, he approached his engagement with war as if it were business. From Batavia, from "a cheaper hotel — (we have moved . . . for the second time) as economy is a vital necessity," he writes:

"On going through my wardrobe, I found that I have a lot of civilian clothes that I shall never use while I am in the Navy, so I have packed them away in one of the K.N.I.L.M. cases & Leyland is taking them back to Australia with his own barang. He will deposit the case in the bank & you can deal with it at your convenience. If it gets lost in transit, put in a claim for £20 for its value under our All Risks Policy — though I don't know whether they will pay up."

Batavia was already being raided by Japanese planes and the siege of Singapore was drawing to its foregone conclusion. He was with intelligence, he must have known that the invasion of the Dutch East Indies could not be far off. But worrying over details — he had written earlier about his life insurance policy — may have been his rational way to stave off fear. Skimming the surface like a water snake.

She moved into her parents' flat in Katoomba, relieved to be free of the enforced monotony of hotel life, yet reluctant. As long as she stayed where he had left her, war seemed temporary, his naval posting a job, as he had said, to meet this temporary upheaval in their lives. In Leura, in the room they had shared, she could feel the link with him and he would know where she was, as if her being there, waiting, could charm him back.

But her parents worried about her. Money was getting low, nothing had yet materialized from his Navy stipend, and things looked bad for Singapore. Be sensible, her father urged, do what Charles would advise doing if she could only discuss it with him (what if there are air raids? her mother asked, and you expecting). That was always the trump card, that and the whispered plea to spare her father any unnecessary strain.

Between walls of sunfaded wallpaper (rosebud print), her father huddled in his habitual place by the radio, intent on the news, irritated if any sound obscured a word, his bald head glistening with concentration. Her mother making florid nervous gestures with teacups and biscuits, Esme whispering to her to be

28

quiet, all of it futile against the steady stream of events. JAPAN ADVANCES AGAIN IN MALAYA. EVACUATION OF IPOH (goodbye to Pritchards and weekend shopping there, goodbye to the incense dark of the Ipoh caves with their monks and shrine niches).

To imagine them there is to situate them within a narrative that bombarded them daily by radio and newsprint. RETREAT FROM KUALA LUMPUR (lorries full of British troops, muddied Rolls-Royces, Red Cross ambulances, steam-rollers, tractors pulling tin dredges — English, Scottish, Australian, Indian, Malay, Chinese drivers at the wheel — a rout). Churchill had promised air support, Churchill said he had absolutely no doubt as to the outcome of the war. SINGAPORE RAIDED BY AIR. She's a fortress, Viktor assured them. They'll fight to the last man. And every one of them doomed, Esme thought. HEAVY BOMBING OF SINGA-PORE. JAPANESE WITHIN 50 MILES OF JOHORE CAUSEWAY (practically at the back gate — and all those gun batteries at the front, facing stupidly out to sea).

Charles wrote from the Hotel de Hoog:

"The news from Singapore is incredibly bad & I feel most anxious for all my friends there. Poor Dorothy — she must be terribly worried. We can only hope & pray that the fate of Hong Kong will not be repeated in Singapore."

—

A slow whiff of smoke thins to nothing from the incense match which is burning itself out on a miniature sampan with its freight of ashes. Who do i burn incense for? Each descent into memory (poling through murky waters) stirs up the dead. Stirs their words to the surface where they blow like ashes suddenly wind-struck. The words i've heard, the phrases i seem to remember, part of a background that shaped me, take on a glow of meaning i never sensed. To make this strange composition, fiction and memory so interlaced it is difficult to tell the difference.

And all the while this high-tech war drags on — impersonal, systematic, it narrows our focus. When the war story is on there is only counting and killing. So many ships blown up. So many planes shot down. Disputes about the so many on each side.

All of us caught in the story, trying to read between the lines, we don't meet the same fatality. These daily bulletins of war declare the real, necessary and willed. What will those who actually live through the "smart bombs," the intricate laser-work of missiles go on remembering? And those who merely live with the news. . . ?

—

There were other stories, ghost stories that conversations would unaccountably veer toward. Datuk kong stories of the power in certain places, hostile or friendly, seeping out at this bend in the road or that house. The spirit power of those who had once lived there. And the colonial fascination with what was other, what preceded them, what kind of power was it that could evade their rational control? At night, sitting with drinks in easy chairs, cigarettes flaring into a darkness thick with day smells, when the trees stirred in the first of the night breezes and bats began their silent lunging overhead, they talked about the houses up the hill, the ones with missing tiles and broken shutters. They retold stories of men equipped with guns who tried to investigate complaints about odd sounds or lights emanating from these places, men who went mad, who found themselves bodily transported outside. Until the hair on the back of the neck stood up and every sense, alerted in the dark, called for something mundane, another round of drinks, a feeble joke tossed off.

Dorothy and Brian were always part of these conversations. Dorothy would urge Brian to retell the story of his club mate, a barrister who, on a dare, had tried to spend the night in one of these houses and woke in the jungle, stumbling around stark naked except for his socks. In the wave of uneasy laughter that followed, Dorothy, reaching for her drink, remarked: It's quite clear that pain and grief live on, even disembodied. And in the silence that followed — I suppose nothing ever ends really.

Dorothy of the jingling bracelets and gorgeous smile. She never seemed to let the heat get her down, nor the endless mahjong parties with their prescribed social ranking. She continued to prod resident matrons and newly arrived wives alike. Concerned about the infant mortality rate, she organized a small group of women to petition the Commissioner for enforcement of the law against urinating in public drains. Don't you ever get tired of always wanting to improve things? Peggy asked caustically. But Esme admired her. Dorothy always seems such a happy person, she told Charles one evening, she never seems to have any doubts.

Esme had doubts. In the glimpses she had of life in the kampongs she sensed a way of being in and of the island she would never experience, despite its flowers that filled her house. As for the urban Chinese, they had been eating, chatting, sleeping, and doing business in their streets for more generations than the British, with all their notions of hygiene, could count. But she didn't say this, didn't know how to say these things that felt like glimpses rather than positions she could take in conversation.

Now she missed those streets with their human currents that swirled in a hubbub of different languages, motley of sarongs, saris, pyjamas, crazy traffic of anything that ran, or walked. The streets themselves a kind of sea, she thought, bearing you up and transporting you almost against your will. Like the sea, full of life and always surging. She remembered the reports they'd heard of Georgetown's reaction to the Japanese bombing. Instead of taking cover in drains and behind pillars, people had rushed out to gaze up at the explosive noise in the sky — it might have been fireworks at the Waterfall Gardens, it might have been the opening of a celestial business, complete with lion dance and firecrackers. But it was the bombing of a population unacquainted with fear, or at least fear of dive-bombers and the sudden machine-gunning of crowded streets. Over a thousand killed.

She couldn't imagine Penang Road pitted with craters, bombed-out buildings, smashed bangsai stalls. She couldn't imagine the bloodied bodies. People ran amok, her father said. Now if you'd become a nurse, my girl, you'd be tending the injured with no squeamishness about it — blown-off legs, shot-up faces and all. Viktor, her mother protested, must you? Well she was never cut out to be a nurse, that's clear. And he opened his paper with unnecessary noise. End of discussion.

She seethed at the way he passed judgement, at the way her mother tried to smooth things over, not wanting, herself, to face the grisly details which she knew he pronounced only to shock and so prove he was right.

This old battleground between them: her desire for training, his for her leisure, the mark of her class. And what if he were right? Squeamish was such a horrid word. No, she had what it took, she thought, to face a crisis. The trouble was worrying about it beforehand, dreading its arrival. And what could she do but dread these days?

And so there was the constraint of finishing tea, stiffly, passing the last of the Jaffa biscuits, wiping her mouth on the serviette before getting up to help Mother with the plates, the washing up she did herself now, and all the time wanting to rush out into the street, howling at the unfairness of it all. War. And what of those women who'd managed to get to Singapore and decided to stay there, stick it out to the end with their husbands? That kind of courage. What was Peggy doing now? Still meeting for coffee at Robinson's, displaying her baby over petits fours? Putting a brave face on it, playing mahjong with other wives holed up in The Raffles? And what if the hotel itself took a direct hit? Could she stand it? The game of keeping up morale, stacking your dragons and your winds in neat little walls, while the real walls were falling all around you — surely they'd have a bomb shelter. But where? Under the dance floor, under the Palm Court where the waiters in their high-buttoned tunics would hardly be standing by? Panic, smoke, people rushing out to get the last food in the shops. No difference between mem sahib and servant.

Well not quite. Asia for Asians, the Japanese said. Propaganda, her father snorted. It's more like Asia for the Japs if you ask me. After the atrocities they've committed in China, do you think the Chinese are going to welcome them with open arms?

But she remembered the look on Amah's face after she'd had to sack Kuki when it became clear what the "mistakes" in the kitchen, the dropped plates, the salt in place of sugar, were all about. She tried to explain trachoma, how contagious it was, how you couldn't have someone with that disease preparing food. Would he go to the clinic? Kuki wore a doomed look, turning his face with those crusted lids and sore red eyes away from her. Days later, days of stony silence on Amah's part, when she'd asked what was the matter, Amah had merely glanced at her and stated the obvious, Kuki good cook. She'd had to repeat the business about contagion because obviously Amah hadn't understood. But now she thought it was she who hadn't understood — he was a good cook to you, Mem, yes, a good cook and you turned him out like an old dog. Not that the rest of it was said — after all she was the Mem.

But you're hardly running a hospice, darling, you're running a household, her mother had soothed. You must never let your servants get the upper hand. He could have gone to the hospital, he could have gone to one of our clinics.

So she had done the right thing, though it was difficult to know sometimes what the right thing was. Her father's absolute assertion: never mind what they tell you about Chinese medicine, it's all superstition. But the idea of having your eyelids rolled back on steel pins so a coldly clinical stranger could daub away at that painful crust . . . What if there were another way? This occurred to her now as she thought about war. What has happened to all the grey areas?

—

Grey, not a word that holds colour even by that name, especially through the greenest eyelet we could find, as if there might be no membrane between indoors and out, as if windows open, even in winter, for the nearest cedar dripping rain and the dawn to step through, might waft us beyond the constraints of ordinary waking. Halfclosed lids, open only a slit to check for light, to sleep-guess time in these borderline mornings, i see your closed ones, that's all.

34

The rest i know by feel, by smell only, the soporific of your skin i curl towards, savouring (as if to keep), this deep we sleep the whole night through, belly to bum, round to round, immense the glow your body makes hallowing mine. Then, slow fade in the racket geese begin, pursuing and being pursued, scooting a splash of noise to make me come to, you not here turning (blue, bluest of eyes) to ask, what time is it?

I write you, wish you, think you here so i won't have to relive our desultory telephone calls, sparse with the details of each day and so thin on love. It's difficult for you to find a private place to call me from, you say, and i am not supposed to call you. I feel your body fading into the track of intentions occupying where you are now.

So, from here to there: "missing you." A letter i might send except that i wouldn't be able to explain this dread that colours memory. Not just the war and its more general dread — the way Bush keeps pronouncing Saddam as Satan with a *d*, underlining apocalyptic fears so he can conjure "a new world order" against "a pan-Arab jihad." I suspect the dread i feel is closer to home.

Home. You ask for news of it and i tell you the robins are back, but even as i'm telling you i hear you drift to some other centre. Dread you would say is the price one pays for not taking a stand. Pro-war or anti-war. For you this is another Vietnam, stacked in much the same way. Yellow ribbons confronting un-American "yellow-bellies."

I think of your sapsuckers mining for nectar in the woody skin of trees, your delight in them, and i envy beings without words.

—

She waited anxiously to hear from Ruth once the Leylands had arrived in Sydney, waited for a first-hand report on Charles.

What was really going on apart from what he said in his letters? Time seemed so fragile now, made up of a sequence of brief immediacies that led nowhere she wanted to imagine.

Dorothy wrote to her from Melbourne: "By remarkable coincidence I ran into Wyn Jolly outside my bank — who seems to be managing quite well on her own with the children. She had just received a note from Mrs. Leyland in Batavia, which is how I know where you are and that you are expecting — what wonderful news, my dear! Despite these awful times, new life must make its way.

"I do worry about Brian. Leyland ran into him in Singapore, in Chinatown of all places, with one of his mates from the Volunteers — looking rather done in I gather. No doubt he has had an awful time of it. I don't suppose much mail is getting through, even if he has had a chance to write.

"I was fortunate enough to find a Navy Office job, which keeps me going. How are you getting along? Do write."

Awful, she thought, feeling lucky to be getting Charles' letters. And how like Dorothy to comment on her pregnancy with such large-mindedness and only then reveal her worries about Brian. So here we are, three stranded wives with husbands fighting a war and still we're "managing" or "getting along" somehow. At least Dorothy and Wyn are in touch — who else from Penang has ended up in Melbourne?

Still, she was glad to be alone with her loneliness. It meant she could focus, she could keep Charles alive with her thoughts winging across the Australian desert, across Western Australia, across the Timor Sea to Java where he sat in a hotel between watches writing to her.

36

If only she could see into the future — perhaps it was better not to know — a tippéd up sherry glass moving with uncanny directness from letter to letter. A name suddenly recognizable, someone dead who was trying to warn them with words spelled out in agonizing slowness. This was before they had even thought about war.

Babies are a wager against death, she thinks, wondering how Dorothy feels, having no bodily trace of Brian. The question of babies had somehow never come up with Dorothy, who had been thinking perhaps, as they all had, there was all the time in the world and always a future.

—

Rain drums its sound around and over the house in early morning light. Water pours from the gutter, an incessant splashing down to rain buckets which are full, have been full for days and brimming over into gravel. When it rains like this, a tangible skin seems drawn around the house, enclosing the cat and me in our plentiful world. Clocks could mean anything and the green light of morning wells incessant through glass.

Hard to imagine the desert "a tactician's dream," ideal for tank warfare the Canadian Institute of Strategic Studies says. In these days of heavy censorship, the media turn to experts for news. Two inch caps, TOOLS OF WAR, flag a page that looks like something torn from a catalogue with its drawings of tanks, missiles, fighters, their names (Tomcat, Harrier) and capabilities. Only the price tag missing. This war which they said would be over quickly, as they say of all wars, is moving on to ground offensives.

A wet morning here and the war there in the late afternoon of the desert — they coexist. Antitank shells and the charred remains of men after their tanks explode. "When one of those rounds comes barrelling through," an expert from the Mackenzie Institute explains, "the crew will be like eggs in an automobile accident." "Crew" meaning "people" — a term to erase the being of ordinary men who once had lives larger than a metal cavity filled with the noise of gun recoil, the sweat of fear.

And to think it's all for oil, you say with disgust into the phone, as twilight wanes serenely across the lake. And i am caught in the echoes of an earlier war, caught in the meshes of defending brutality to stop brutality. Tuned to a consuming serial drama, we begin to think like them as the space around us fills with controversy —

Then how could we trace our fingers over skin with its delicate opening of pores as our bodies respond, frond by frond, uncurling in the wet? How could i plant my hand around your breast, suck your nipple into grandeur as we spilled into luxuriant time, no-time, just the gulf of an island — when this continues over there, this trapped dying among those driven to war.

It's clear that nothing is over, Dorothy said. We leave our imprints like weather, a set of atmospheric conditions another *we* will live within. The weather of doorways, of windows, disturbing a room. An altered temperature, another zone you feel halfway up the road . . . ghosts who can't leave the scene of their interrupted loves and intentions.

—

The flat in Katoomba was nothing like the spacious houses they were used to with their high ceilings, open balconies and windows over which the Boy would quietly unroll rattan chicks as day intensified its glare outside. In these rooms, warmth lay stagnant between walls close with cooking smells, damp laundry (always undies or socks to dry), coloured by the smoke from Viktor's intermittent cigars — compensation, he said, for the cigarettes he'd been forced to give up.

Esme watched the pallor leave his face as his sense of humour returned. You've been doing him a world of good, her mother whispered. But the chuckle she might induce would still end, as often as not, in a coughing fit. She hated seeing him low. Even more she hated his denial of it, the calling-up of his authoritative self being only shadow play. At moments she glimpsed a father she didn't know and watched him covertly to discover who he was. Aware of her glance, he would look away or utter some brusque comment to throw her off.

Still, despite the new, what was it? air of squalor so extraordinary for them, it was like putting on old clothes to be back with them after almost four years of marriage. The same patterns of conversation, same sore points, but still a comfort just being there. Mother's strength has increased as Dad's has waned, she realized, watching her mother busy at the sink. Where were the lace hankies drenched in cologne? Where were the gorgeously excessive hats and scarves? A layer had been peeled back, exposing a mother practical in ways she had not suspected.

And yet there was something familiar about this too, something she almost remembered — what? That brief time in London before her parents had returned to India and she and her younger brother had been packed off to boarding school. Troublesome, always the "bad one," she had been discovered by her uncle at the tube station in the very act of running away. What she remembered missing was her ayah's soft voice and endlessly forgiving arms with the bracelets one could slip up and down, over and over, Ayah who had always slept on the floor of the nursery beside her bed. Ayah who had been hired to be forgiving. She had no clear memories of her mother in London except for the word Pneumonia and her father's black bag sitting on the table in the hall. Dark wallpaper, dark wainscot, doors closing her out.

Now, with a baby on the way and the pittance of a Navy wife's allowance — well, you simply must learn a few things, her mother announced. There ensued an initiation, not without a few disasters, into the mysteries of cooking.

Leather of eggs? Viktor enquired, fork poised over a dismal soufflé. She couldn't tell whether the tears that pricked her eyes were from rage or self-pity. Never mind, darling, Aylene patted her hand, expecting makes one emotional. Rage, definitely rage.

Because of the drought, they could only do their laundry and bathe between certain hours in the morning and evening. Scrubbing at stained armholes as she bent over the tub, she remembered the deliciousness of water sounds, whether a soft trickle as Kabun dampened the orchids hanging over their terrace or a bright splashing as Syce poured bucketfuls on the car. Water, endless water, and in somebody else's hands.

Gradually, as Viktor's strength increased, they managed occasional rounds of golf. Lingering by sand traps — to improve her swing he said, to let him catch his breath she thought — he would reminisce about other fairways, or chuckle, good show, when she managed to retrieve a sorry performance. Then in the gum tree scent of a Katoomba morning she felt that shy affection she had felt for him, for them, when she had first come out from school to Malaya, both of them delighted with the attractive girl their daughter had become.

"Ugly duckling turned swan," she scribbled to a friend, allowing herself to gloat, just a little, after her miserable time at school. And then, to be honest — "I'm afraid they don't know the duck is only hiding under all these extravagant feathers." They bought her a complete wardrobe, showed her off to everyone, showed her everything, from the Raffles Hotel in Singapore to the temple caves at Ipoh. "The trio" she wrote with pride on the back of a photograph enclosed with the letter. Aylene, Esme, Viktor, posed with Paddy the dog under the sweeping portico of their Malacca house, she in her new tropical costume, standing between her parents but a little closer to Viktor, feet in white pumps primly together, empty hands at her sides, the back of her left hand almost touching the back of his right, the one without the cigarette.

Only after he had been posted to Penang and they had resettled there did the allure of life in the tropics begin to pall. She grew tired of her mother's attempts to dress her for an endless round of social engagements, all obligatory — But the mauve, darling, is so much more attractive than that rather drab beige. It's called champagne, Mother! Or her father's terse comments about the young men who littered the hall tray with their calling cards — You'd better give young Farquarson the cold shoulder, I hear he has a weakness for Asiatic girls. She had rather liked Farquarson.

Now she remembered all too vividly the irritations of that hemmed-in world that Charles had saved her from, dear Charles, with his earnest face and uproarious laugh, a laugh so unlike her father's. Charles who had no pretensions, who would joke about her mother's initial comment (later denied): Darling, he's very nice but he's only a rubber clerk.

After they were married she discovered that he wrote home every week, letters that were chatty, humorous, the kind she

41

couldn't imagine writing to her own parents (she read snatches as she bent over his shoulder to kiss him). Yes, she was curious, especially about his mother to whom, she felt, the letters were really addressed. A Flora she would never meet who died in England during their first year together. It hadn't been easy, his grief. The grief of an only child raised by a mother he protected during those long years of the Great War when his father fought in the trenches and then recovered in hospital.

In the wake of her death he withdrew from Esme and she knew he was regretting their honeymoon in Brastagi, grieved that it replaced the leave at home he would otherwise have taken. She couldn't help resenting this, his first betrayal she felt, as if there would be others. But then she reminded herself that it was he, he who was feeling bereft. Still, it was difficult to forgive, despite love — or perhaps because of it. She wanted Charles to herself. He was the first really decent thing that had happened to her.

—

Who's this, Mummy? Your grandmother on your father's side. What was she like? I never met her — your father was extremely fond of her.

A story involving certain feelings gets passed on in an intonation, a hesitation, a gap between two sentences.

To remember (what is memory, what invention?) seems to involve re-listening. Not a repeat so much as a puzzling out of intuitions, senses, glimpses of a larger context. The world they lived in, a tempo, a texture not even they could describe though they were in the midst of it, survives in odd fragments, bits of film, carefully collected snaps, stories that barely suggest what lies behind them.

Making waffles, pouring melted butter into milk in this West Coast kitchen, why should i be visited suddenly by the smell of new cloth at the Chinese tailor's in Penang? Memory, a flash, flush of sensation through the body. Unbidden. The only time she took me with her to wait while she tried on a half-made evening gown, adjustments, a sleeve to be lengthened, bodice refitted. Yards of white gathered at her waist, the smell of new cloth, her showing me what the embroidery would look like in its scarlet exuberance. I only have eyes for that creamy flowing, flowering like untouched gardenias round her feet. I think her gorgeous, the tailor, squatting on the floor to pin up the hem as she stands on thin brown paper, properly deferential. Gazing at her, i breathe in the air of his shop, the richness of its smells a batik layering, all the bolts of colour laid out to touch, faded odours of cooking from the back, but most of all the hot scratchy stillness as if the cloth itself were soaking up the air, my waiting, their talking over what she wants. Endless it seems, my staring out between blinds at the usual stream of shoppers, loiterers, hawkers, everything slowing down so that i see the teacups on the sidewalk, a bowl of rice, and not the syce-driven cars. See, for just a second, what it might be like to be that girl, younger than me, hanging around the kedai across the way, spoken to and speaking to the others but all the while staring with that territorial rudeness i know, staring between people and cars at me, outsider in her father's? uncle's? shop, while i, guardian of this gorgeous mother, just as rudely stare back.

—

Under the fan, under the scolding of a chichak hanging from the wall above, he attempts to answer her letter. With only a few brief hours to himself, he has taken off his uniform in favour of the familiar cotton pyjamas he greets as a memento of their

together. Easier to write when he feels, however superficially, at home.

"I told myself to put a brave face on it," she has confided, "and
then my courage failed me and I felt in the depths of despair."

"Don't, my pet," he wants to say, he wants to simply take her in
his arms. But, given their situation, knowing what he writes
must stand for everything he cannot do, he takes up his pen:

"When the tide does turn out here in our favour, it will turn
with unexpected rapidity, so don't become depressed about the
future."

Thinking of her carrying it, their future — shouts outside, some
new crisis in the traffic which grows more hectic with each
passing day. He contemplates her face in the familiar snapshot
resting on his table. Sensitive, he thinks. Intelligent. Will she
know that he is partly bluffing? For her sake — and yes, he
admits it, for his own. Still, he can't quite see her a mother,
though the idea excites him. His child in her, a living merger
of their two selves. The embodiment of something that has
always escaped him.

In the midst of teacups and overstuffed brown chairs, their plush
rather worn (this *was* a furnished flat after all), Viktor spoke of
joining the ARP, being "useful" in some way, but Aylene worried
that he wasn't up to hauling a stirrup pump around. You're just
on the mend, my dear, I do think it would be rather foolish.
Esme would have liked to man a stirrup pump herself —
"reduces the life of a bomb from twenty to two minutes without causing violent spluttering of molten material," she read
from the handbook. "The operator should stand behind a wall

44

or a substantial piece of furniture so as not to expose himself to danger from flying molten globules." It all sounds rather exciting, she said, to Aylene's predictable horror — in your condition? — and Viktor's, you're out of your head, my girl.

But he made sure they followed the instructions in the *Herald* for equipping their flat. They were already using black-out curtains, but he checked the list and insisted they purchase whatever they didn't already have: "buckets of dry sand (oh what a shame we're not near the beach, Father), a long-handled shovel — preferably wood, a long-handled Dutch hoe, portable containers filled with water (someone will have to go without a bath, I'm afraid), a pair of household steps, a tomahawk." It sounds like the Wild West, she concluded, what on earth would we use a tomahawk for? You'd better hope to God you don't have to find out, he snapped. Her levity a childish silliness, no doubt.

She glared at the ads in the paper in front of her, hoping to erase him. SMART FROCKS — flaunt a yoke of vivid scarlet to dress up beautiful beige. Smart frocks were for willowy girls with no tummy. ARE YOU HALF THE GIRL YOU USED TO BE? can you do only half the things you used to do? KRUSCHEN TONIC SALTS. Half the girl and twice the size.

She wanted to spray something, anything, with a stirrup pump. Mother-To-Be fights off Japs. Navy Wife defends Unborn Child. Captions for a self she would invent to patch over the hole inside. Captions to counter the other ones in her head: Hopeless Coward. Pregnant Sow. What would Charles think if he could see her? Hands red from washing plates, tummy swollen, waist gone, pimples pushing up the powder on her nose. She felt ugly. Could see it in the way her father barely glanced at her these days, while her mother grew increasingly solicitous.

45

She knew what that meant: her attractiveness gone. Washed up. How did other women manage?

—

One of those misty mornings winter broods in, cloud cover so low we can't see the other shore of the lake. Life slows down in this weather, even the trees seem not to breathe. Only the grass, ribbed with wet as if there had been rain. Air so thick we seem to float in it.

Like the morning we rose, surprised by a shout, that voice again. Resolved to decipher its meaning, you took the trail up to the garden shed, i walked down the drive where it curves close to their fence. Through salal and ironwood, i heard a door open, so close it couldn't be the house but one of their cabins. The same voice, the same monotone of despair tinged with fury at whatever lurks out there abducting one's comfort — so close i could make out the word, "GIN-ger! GIN-ger!"

You won't believe this — it's only a cat, i told you when we met. Someone in one of the cabins must have brought her cat and it's run off. And to think we made up a whole story around the sound of her voice. Later you said, gazing out at the empty screen of window air was, i don't think whatever that woman's calling is even there. It's not a cat, it's something she can't remember.

Even fog retains this voice, like a memory-thread, an inaudible echo in the day. This is a time for drawing close, for wood fires, warm lights, sharing a pot of tea.

But you are visiting your mother encased in fragile widowhood. You will go through her clothes, cleaning the foodstains she no longer notices. You will find the things she has lost, take her to

46

friends she hasn't seen, answer the stack of unanswered cards and notes which loom beyond her ability to respond. And so you keep her connected to the remaining people in her world, wintry farmland drenched with a lifetime of association, draining, now, to one small room. You don't find this easy, your own associations with that world shot through with old betrayals. Yet you can't abandon the mother you feel abandoned you.

Near the end of your visit she will cry because you are leaving again. You will cry too, but you can't stand living anywhere near the claiming currents of that mother-pull. Guilt — "my only daughter" — expectation — "why don't you ever . . ." — and denial — "I don't understand . . ."

So you live on an island in another country with a woman your mother thinks is merely a friend. And the too-much you can't talk about moves in like fog, despite small and unexpected clearings. She is your child now and you must protect her, you say, though you always have. Smothered with responsibility but never mothered enough.

Listen, all the while you are away this land continues to hold us, enfold our life together here, even in our apartness. And yes, of course we invent so much: a home and all it is supposed to make up for. We carry marriage stories in our blood, our mothers' stories shadowing the ones we're trying to invent.

—

She read the news of evacuees from Penang or Singapore. YOUNGEST PENANG REFUGEE. MONTH-OLD BABY IN SYDNEY. "Mrs. Grant Watson and her children left Penang about three days before the Japanese captured the island, abandoning their house, their car, and most of their clothes." Or Mrs. W. L. Waugh who moved into her new house in Penang on December

1st and had to evacuate on December 13th. "The Chinese servants behaved wonderfully during raids — I made them dig a shelter beside the house." She read with a kind of amazement the testimony of survivors, their heroics. Who were most heroic, she wondered, those who left or those, the servants, who were left behind?

There was talk about the evacuation among the expatriates, how poor it looked for Europeans to abandon their Asian business colleagues, their medical and government staff, to the enemy. What else could they do? Aylene asked. You couldn't evacuate the whole island, now could you? Viktor was quiet and Esme wondered what memories of the hospital were running through his mind.

Day by day the relentless narrative of withdrawal made headlines. On February 1st, they heard the news that all surviving Allied troops had withdrawn across the Johore Causeway to Singapore Island, blowing up the bridge behind them. The siege of Singapore had begun, though its governor preferred to use the term "investiture." They listened to news of repeated bombardments, inadequate shelters, looting, fires, and last-minute evacuation of women and children on ships threatened by Japanese mines.

Peggy, she thought. Peggy must be on one of those ships trying to escape. Heavy fire from the air. Torpedoes underwater. Running a gauntlet to get to us sipping tea and listening to the news.

On February 8th, the enemy gained a foothold on the north coast of the island. Days of fighting, strong resistance around Bukit Timah. "The civil population is, from all accounts, standing up to its ordeal with great fortitude." Chaotic reports, the Tengah aerodrome and the racecourse only a few miles from the water reservoirs were directly in the line of advance. Then silence. The war correspondents have all left, Viktor pointed out.

Several days later, he stormed through the door with a late edition of the paper and flung it down on the table: SINGAPORE'S FATE A MATTER OF HOURS. It's over, he said, that's the end of Malaya! Oh no, no it can't be, her mother protested. Esme felt their uselessness as they stood in their aprons gazing stupidly at the brooding capitals. Their other life seemed eerily to retreat. Now there was only this transient apartment in a strange country filled with other people's furniture.

——

After the chaotic queue for the ship, go-downs burning all along the harbour, planes coming in overhead, the fear that now, now at last when you've let him talk you into going for the children's sake, there won't be room, they'll sink the ship in its mooring lines, this last ship, or you'll hit a mine — but none of that happened. Steaming out in a sort of post-sunset — the glare of fire, the pall of smoke — sailing with no lights, you waited, holding your breath, hushing the children, a boatload of women and children smoke-smudged and disarrayed, waiting in fear to breathe again. And you did, you left Singapore to its fate, all the men . . . but there were the children to worry about. You made it out into the Strait, Sumatra somewhere off to the west, stars, a clear night, and everyone settling down in crowded cabin assignments, the children two to a berth or on the floor, their drained exhausted bodies crying out against the strangeness, always this hushing hushing of the child in yourself in your child out there. Then the planes came over and you felt the hit and it was all chaos again but worse, screaming and smoke as the ship tilted, you scrambling up the narrow companionway with others onto the deck, shoving the kids ahead of you to the nearest lifeboat as the crew shouted orders, no one listening or able to in that colossal din of planes and guns — and the lifeboat, which you welcomed like safety, rolls just as it hits water, spilling you into that cold sea, its weight the smack of

49

reality. How clothes drag you down, and where is your youngest whose hand has somehow slipped through yours, or your son, who can barely swim. That panicked loss, fighting water to call their names and nothing clear except big salt gulps as you struggle to kick off your shoes. A woman near you screams she is going to drown — I've lost my children, you scream back, still calling, calling, and the woman goes under for the third time so you grab her, tear at her hands clutching your neck, let go, let go . . . Only hours later, alone, letting the current drift you toward the beach you hear surf splash and tired, too dead tired to care about rocks, you make it through, somehow, over the worst and there's the sand, you dragging yourself against the ebb, not caring but driven to make that final effort on hands and knees, collapse face down still water rocked, when you hear a noise, feel grit in your face, and the clipped impossible syllables of Japanese, at least you think that's what it is, a gun at your back . . . You know that this, this is reality and you've been taken.

—

Miss Macey was commiserating with Mother over their losses, all that had been left behind for the Japs to enjoy. Your beautiful wedding dress, darling! her mother exclaimed, adding a detailed description of the gown, the wedding and the reception, all with appropriate my my's from Miss Macey.

Drab Miss Macey was one of her mother's recently acquired Katoomba friends. Impressed by stories of opulence, she was eager, Esme felt, to trot home the details to friends or family who would laugh at imperious Pommies who had such airs and yet, when the chips were down, had failed to save Singapore.

But Mother, what on earth would a Japanese soldier do with my wedding dress? Her faintly mocking tone might put it all in perspective, she thought, but as soon as the words left her mouth she regretted them.

That you never know, Aylene replied with the air of one declining to mention a horror everyone else freely anticipates.

Bandages? Miss Macey leaned toward Esme. They'd be short of supplies, don't you think?

From the armchair where he had been reading, apparently oblivious to conversation, Viktor snorted. They've over-run all the hospitals and judging by what happened in Hong Kong, they're more likely to shoot patients than dress them.

The savages! Miss Macey recoiled. And to think they're almost on our doorstep.

Byron, you see, was much too sanguine. And taking up the book he declaimed:

> *If thou hadst died as honour dies,*
> *Some new Napoleon might arise,*
>   *To shame the world again —*
> *But who would soar the solar height,*
> *To set in such a starless night?*

And, gazing at them severely over his reading specs: Lord Byron, I'm afraid, could never have imagined an entire army of Bonapartes.

Esme felt the little frisson that shivered through Miss Macey, and, despite herself, exulted in her father's sense of drama. Let the Macey convey that if she could.

But really, what was there to choose between them? she asked herself later in her room. Such useless talk! None of them had a young husband fighting unnamed horrors, let alone whole armies of Bonapartes.

—

Awake with a headache this morning, i listen to sheets of rain closing down the house, an incessant gurgle of gutters. Air hectic this time of year, and dark, though daylight is on the increase. Someone is burning wood — i catch its tang as the wind shifts, and imagine a stove like the one i haven't lit, already warming damp clothes. Who wants to get up on mornings like this?

A night of presences again. Something prowling around the wall, and not raccoons. No clang of garbage cans down the drive as they try to break open the lids. Maybe our complex system of bunjy cords is working.

Whatever came around was closer than that. Something between the wall and my skin. And not concerned with food, though want drives it.

Can what we fear embody itself? Before you left, you cleared your desk to a blank as you always do. Leaving no telltale trace that i might sniff. Yet your clothes are alive, thick with your smell in the closet. I haunt the evidence of what preoccupied you, books you left by our bed, fragmentary lists, telephone messages.

What are you thinking in your mother's room, in the pancake house where you used to meet your friends, on the streets of that small town where you learned to drive? Do you talk about the war with your mother? Or do you refrain, knowing she will never understand your anger? Oh the complex attitudes we bear toward what we come from. A tangled web that leaves us oddly positioned.

It seems to me the wind is shifting, but i can't see how. I can't even remember what we ate the night before you left. And this seems terribly important, like a sign i haven't read.

On February 12th he wrote:

"Life here proceeds fairly normally — we have had a number of alerts but no bombs. By the time you read this, Batavia may be a target for Japanese attacks, but you must not worry yourself for my safety. You must have faith, with me, that with God's protection I shall come through it all in safety."

By the time she read it, the Japanese had invaded Sumatra and seized Palembang — seventy-five percent of the oil supplies for the Dutch East Indies. And the ships: thirty-two of them, warships and transports including evacuation boats all heading for Batavia, sunk, damaged or forced aground. Java was clearly next.

He wrote about their friends: "I do hope that Brian, Glen — and oh! so many others we know, will come out of it all and live to reap some benefit for the sacrifices they are now making. How thankful you must be that I did not reach Singapore!"

—

Later, when we moved up the Hill to Camville, the tall, sensible-looking house built by a wealthy Chinese and surrounded by jungle, there were monkeys in the trees, troupes of them ranging from babies with unblinking eyes to granddaddies shaking the wire on top of the chicken pen with malign glee. They moved like aerialists, leaping trees, swinging down onto the roof of the summerhouse, scattering from the lawn with wild curses at the dog's forays. We could hear them coming through the leaves long before we saw them.

And the bats were outdoors, not hanging by their claws like so many wrinkled packages from the ceiling of the back stairs.

No more daring each other to stand in the dark, slamming the door so their papery wings would stir in a rush of unwrapping above us. Here they swooped about outside long after we were safely tucked in bed.

No mosquito netting, no durian tree, no ghost.

—

Impatient, sweating — twenty minutes before he was supposed to go on duty and no sign of his clean uniform — he paced from table to bed. Hang it all, the fellow had seemed shiftless from the first. But then dhobis were as hard to find as taxis in a Batavia engorged with refugees. Odd how something as simple as a dhobi's failing to appear should trigger his apprehension about the war and Batavia's situation.

Glancing at Esme's portrait, he smiled grimly. I've been doing very well, he thought, keeping my eye on ciphers. He picked up the photo — it had been taken in a Penang studio by a Chinese photographer, a good one. He knew the embossed name in the lower corner, could see the shop on Chulia Street.

If she were here now she'd be fuming over the dhobi's wanton unreliability. She was very good with the servants. Once she felt in the right, she didn't mince words. Yet she could take their side too. He'd come home one afternoon to find her seething over the Catholic priest who'd just paid a visit to one of their servants. Well, she wasn't their servant exactly, that Tamil girl living with their kabun — a lovely young thing, but Catholic and unmarried and about to give birth to her first child. No possibility of marriage — Kabun's official wife was still in India. Not an uncommon story for migrant labourers. But the two of them had seemed happy together.

Then the priest came to chastise his lost sheep, tell her she was living in a state of sin. Esme sent him packing but all her anger couldn't retrieve the girl who died not long after of some mysterious ailment. Esme blamed the priest. He damned her, she said, and insisted on it despite his rational arguments.

Then there was that odd occurrence on the upstairs verandah. He'd been at the office, but Esme and someone — was it Peggy? he couldn't remember — were having tea on the lawn. Wyn, or was it Peggy? glanced up and asked, who is that lovely Tamil girl? Esme had seen her too and said she looked rather sad despite her brilliant sari and the temple flowers in her hair.

—

If gazing at his image would bring him back alive, she would practise that magic fervently, memorizing the photo he sent of himself in uniform, reading and rereading his face for signs of what he had been thinking at the moment it was taken. Such a formal pose, shot from the left, the fingers of his left hand resting lightly on the back of his right, the braid on his left sleeve more prominent than either hand. He looked very serious under the peak of his officer's cap with its naval crest. His eyes seemed distant, contemplating a future she couldn't see. Was he thinking about her at all? Even the smallest suggestion? No, he looked every inch an officer, steady, keen — why hadn't she seen this side of him before? But there, just there if you looked in the corner of his eye, a hint of amusement.

She tried to remember his mouth, the mouth that looked stern in the photo but was, she knew, remarkably sensitive. She tried to remember the particular light in his eyes as he leaned toward her . . . No, he was already close, holding her close on the dance floor — the Runnymede, the Club, it didn't matter. She

55

could smell his cigarettes, the odour of pomade on his hair, the freshly laundered Egyptian cotton he wore, and under it, his slightly damp skin. She inhaled it, all of it, her nose just touching his neck above the collar — it didn't matter what the others thought. He held her, guiding her with that careful pressure of his hand on the small of her back, sheltering her as they glided through a crowd that seemed to recede . . .

And yet there always was *a Veil past which I could not see* . . . How did it go? *Some little talk awhile of* ME *and* THEE — then what? — *and then no more of* THEE *and* ME. Of course. Khayyám.

You've always been a brooder, Aylene said, you only end up making yourself miserable.

She'd always been? Her mother who barely knew her, who had left her all those years in boarding school, what would she know about hiding in a cupboard, losing herself in a book so she wouldn't have to engage in the battle that was field hockey, girls she knew transformed into shin-bashing furies. No team pride, they said, no self-control. Yet she was the one who memorized whole poems when she had to walk alone at the end of the school file.

Forewarned is forearmed, Jenks used to say when she had skipped yet another practice. We'll see how much you like to be alone . . . And it was not that she'd ever gone begging for punishment.

—

This new obsession with high-tech fighters and tanks: charms against evil, against the threats of a "mad-man" who spent $50 billion on armaments in the last decade but is not considered mad for that reason. Mad because he takes on the world's

mightiest power, this two-bit dictator invoking "the Mot
Battles." And our media repeat his rhetoric so they can cel
the American arsenal (equipped of course with Canadian com-
ponents — yes, Lori, i read that too). You see, i carry on these
conversations in my head . . .

And today, today . . . Dew not frost this morning, wet on the
leaves. A tangible smell of earth, a string of Canada geese
honking their arrival with the sun:

91 CHILDREN AMONG 288 BODIES RECOVERED IN RUBBLE, Iraq
reports in the wake of American bombing, of — what? Language floats. An air raid shelter, Iraq asserts. Military bunker,
the U.S. counter-reports. Disputed terms echoing back and
forth across communication waves. A CNN print displays pain-
fully small bodies wrapped in blankets, blurred figures bending
on the street to fold back a corner, confirm the unthinkable.

"I suppose the suggestion that he may have indeed encouraged
civilians to occupy what he knew to be a military facility is
possible," the U.S. Secretary of Defense defensively purports.

Oh Lori, the disgust and pain i feel today must resemble yours.
Today you are visiting your aunt and i can't even call to talk
about it.

———

As she stared at his photo for the hundredth time, it drained of
all familiarity and became merely a picture of a man in uniform.
She could not remember how his skin smelled. There were only
disconnected images: ears sticking out as he brushed the sides
of his head with the silver brushes she had given him; white
legs, a bit knobby-kneed below his woollen bathing suit; head
thrown back in an uproarious laugh as they stood bundled up

57

with friends on the slope of Mount Kosciusko — disarming. Unthinking.

She struggled to rally a memory that would bring him to her living and whole, called herself a traitor as she lay across her useless bed.

Java had fallen — almost a week ago and still no word. She wrote to the Navy office in Melbourne, requesting information, but she knew that if he had arrived safely in Australia he would have telegrammed.

Darling, you must pull yourself together, Aylene said. You don't want all this to affect the baby.

She sat numbly by the window, convinced the widows' station they were building in Sydney for trains bringing in the war dead loomed ahead of her. She could imagine the rows of canvas-wrapped bodies on the platform . . . No, not even that was real.

All she had left was this child whose kicks, small flutters at first, were gaining insistence. A future without a future, fatherless. To think that with a child on the way, he had gone off like that — thoughtless and heroic, throwing his life away for the sake of his country. What was a country anyway? She had never had one.

II

IT HAD BEEN more for reasons of secrecy than economy that he and his friend Matson had moved to the Hotel de Hoog. Assigned to codes and ciphers, they had difficulty balancing the need for secrecy with the natural camaraderie that ensued whenever they ran into refugees from Malaya. Moving to a Dutch hotel where they were surrounded by a language they couldn't speak seemed the simplest course of action. Here he could snatch breakfast after a few hours sleep and reflect for a moment over a solitary cup of tea.

Unfortunately the woman beaming across the room at him, a handsome woman with two young daughters and an affable husband, could in fact speak English. Two days ago the Vander-Haeghes had been delighted to practise their English on him. He had a quick drink with them, managing to evade questions as to why he was in Batavia and not at sea. People would rather tell their own stories anyway, which, for now, was highly convenient. It had been easy enough to chaff the girls about their flight from Sumatra one step ahead of the Japs. And to wish them well (rather hollowly, he felt). But today he could not play dumb. Nodding briefly in their direction, he busied himself with toast and marmalade. His poor waiter had finally got used to serving these essentials at all hours of the day — just when it was too late.

The battle for the Java Sea, an unequal contest to begin with, was over. Remaining R.N. staff, except for Matson and himself, had moved south of the city into the mountains at Bandoeng. Word was still coming through from Pilchard to stay at their post, but he knew that the Japanese had landed at Surabaya and would shortly be in possession of the northern coastline. He and Matson had strict orders to burn everything before leaving, all evidence of their work, but if they had to wait much longer how would they get out? He hoped their people at Bandoeng would have the sense to give removal orders before bombing decimated the rail line.

He hated this waiting. But then he, at least, had information. Glancing around the dining room with its quiet groups of people — tense, he thought, though nobody's showing it — he wondered how many of them, like the Vander-Haeghes, were still hoping for an evacuation ship. It was extraordinary how people clung to habitual patterns right up to the last moment. Conversation was for the most part unintelligible to him but gestures were not. He saw the same passing of cups, the same pouring of coffee or tea that he imagined anyone looking in at the house on Peel Avenue would have seen Esme and himself engaged in several months ago.

Sometimes when he thought back to Penang, everything that had occurred in the interim felt like some adventure flick that he had accidentally stepped into, caught up in a role already written for him. This long view would open only on occasional moments, for overriding it was a sense of outrage, of challenge even, as he and Matson spent hours decoding and transmitting the terse data of war.

*It was the band of bananas — you don't talk about these things — it was
the band of bananas that brought it home. you can't speak about it — only
just ripe, and so many of them, enough to give you several bites each, the
whole thing hanging so ripe, so unbearably heavy. your feet wrapped up in
rags, the sight of you! pilfered sarongs, mismatched bits of clothing,
haggard, no combs, carrying broken crockery like prized possessions from
the house they'd let you loot. mouth still sore from hours in the sea, you can
barely swallow, but the bananas — you can't speak of this so that anyone
could understand — a perfect yellow, smelling dearly familiar, smelling of
food in that jungle clearing they'd marched you through. smelling of some
other life, not this one newly acquired, not fear, not pain, not the bayonets.
all they'd given you was a little broken rice, and all you can think is waste,
the lost children, dead babies who will never taste banana, and that woman
shuffling beside you like a sleepwalker — you can't speak of it to her, you
can't break through her pain.*

*Yes, but there is your hunger, you are still alive and there are the bananas,
a whole band of them ripe for taking, though none of you could possibly
carry it. Mrs. G., with that imperious gesture you know so well, Mrs. G.
who imagines herself your intercessor, has the guard slice it off the tree and
haul it up on his shoulder like somebody's kabun. he does it and you are not
surprised. but then when you get to the building in Muntok, he walks off
with it, and when Mrs. G. objects another soldier beats her with his rifle.
watching the shock on her face you see that's how it is — you are prisoners
now who have merely offered him his due.*

They sat in the Navy office staring at the message Matson had
just received. That's it, that's the order, he said — but they're
telling us to head for Cilapcat!

Don't worry, old boy. If they think we're immortal we'll jolly well have to be.

Matson looked sick. Good god, don't they know that nothing's got past those subs for days now? He could feel Matson's despair, Matson who, at the end of his watch, must be tired out.

Look, he stubbed his cigarette with a decisive air, if that's where the Bandoeng people are going, that's where we're going. Let's get a move on.

Now that they were leaving their enforced limbo, panic hovered. There seemed a score of split-second decisions to make, what to destroy, what to take — not their kit in the hotel, no time for that when Matson discovered what was possibly the last train was due to leave in an hour and a half. Charles made sure that every record, every scrap of cipher work was burnt to ash in the barrel they'd nicked while Matson dashed off to round up survivors from the Java Sea who'd straggled into Batavia over the last few days. By Jeep, by rickshaw they got down to the station only to find the train late and no one sure when it would actually leave. Hours later, hours of reflection on what they'd left undone or might have done or might have to do, they boarded an overcrowded and clearly final train.

—

it had been a cinema — you couldn't quite see all of it from your position on the concrete floor, sitting with the others, so many others, through the hot, sweltering night thick with the smells of exhausted bodies, no room to stretch out. you were sitting among the women, back to back with your mother, you felt her head drop as she drifted into an uncomfortable doze, and sometimes you wanted to leap up and scream how can you sleep? but then you made yourself sit still, you thought about the others, the wounded ones, the bleeding ones who groaned so awfully — a child whining not far from you, his mother giving him a smack — the servicemen in shabby uniforms talking low or sagging where they sat.

you are wide awake with the hollow feel of hunger and your cramped position. awake so you can wonder — that torn poster on the wall they shoved you past — some warrior coiled to strike, some shimmering lady with a very white face. at home you'd never been allowed in the Chinese cinema though you'd wondered what it would be like, what you would see flickering up there on the screen. now there is only the cluster of doctors and nurses working on a low platform, doing what you're not quite sure — but you can hear the occasional ripping of cloth — Chinese tablecloths from Singapore, someone told your mother, embroidered pillowcases. you watch their shadows on the empty screen as they bend and straighten and bend again, a different kind of picture show, accompanied by those awful groans which rise and drop like applause — you think you shouldn't think such things.

—

Now that the train had been moving for some time, leaving padi fields for the steep grade into the mountains, their sense of panic began to fade. They were on the move with a fighting chance at escape, although the possibility of derailment from a bombed-out line, or even sudden attack, seemed likely. So it was still a waiting game, even if they were in motion.

Leaning his head against the wooden sash, he gazed at the jungle slipping by. No way of seeing ahead. Jungle was still jungle — they could be passing the ancient boulders, the unwavering green of Sumatra. The guesthouse he knew so well at Brastagi could be just around the next bend, or Sibajak's volcanic cone filmed with cloud and rising like some apparition. Hard to imagine it enemy territory. He'd always had a sense of physical lightness, clarity even, in the free space of those mountains.

The euphoria he and Brian had shared on Senaboeng, waving their hats at the bird's eye view of jungle spread below them.

Brastagi was one of "his" places, though Esme thought it all rather wild and disappointing when he took her there. She wasn't one for climbing mountains and even the ponies failed to appeal. A bit of a disaster, that, he thought, smiling wryly at the memory. Matson caught his eye and grinned from his crooked position, one shoulder bearing the weight of an exhausted AB slumped beside him. Their train was slowing to a crawl around a particularly torturous curve. Think we'll make Bandoeng? Matson mouthed.

No worries, he grinned back, using some of the Australian lingo they'd begun to imitate between themselves. He felt a surge of affection for Matson, for the men in the carriage, some of whom he knew had been through hell. Still, we're the lucky ones — if luck stays with us. He pushed the thought of Singapore into a deep recess — think of that later. Luck was it? or Providence? He hesitated at the notion of God — it seemed egotistical somehow to assume a personal Hand in their affairs.

—

when they ordered you into the padang, so fast you had to leave food behind, counted you over and over in the scorching sun — when they took your scissors, the jewellry you couldn't hide — when they brought in the Dutch prisoners with all their barang, well-fed and suitably dressed — when they separated the men and marched them off at bayonet point, no time for goodbyes —

or when they ordered you up the hill to bungalows with no water, no fuel, each one housing some twenty-four of you counting the children, crammed in garages even, barbed wire fence, guard-house at the gate — that was it, wasn't it? or the vegetable truck tipping its rotten contents onto the road to

66

be sorted through, or the meat truck, and the guard retrieving what was left
from the dogs, hacking the meat into bits, one chewed-up bit for each
bungalow, less than a taste, a greasy residue — and you found yourself
housed with strangers, women you wouldn't ordinarily speak to, let alone
share a pot of rice with. but there you were chopping charred roofbeams
together for firewood, and with two dull axes — was that when you knew
that everything had changed, and irreversibly?

or was it when they gave you chungkals to tackle the sewage drains that
had backed up? those brute-heavy hoes and you wading into the filth, stench
so strong it would knock you back, but having to get the drains unplugged
and knowing the others who were fanning fires or picking rice from the grit
and broken glass were counting on you — and then when that filth began
to move, the small wry satisfaction you felt: taken, yes, but not completely.

—

They walked into Bandoeng in pouring rain, having been
assured that the break in the line would be repaired by dawn.
It was difficult to take the assurance seriously, although the
engineer seemed confident that he could round up a local
work-gang. The break had occurred only a mile or two short
of town.

Stumbling down the line in torrential dark with only a couple
of torches, the hammering of rain on leaves all around them,
they gradually saw Bandoeng's lights flicker through the wet.
The possibility of towels, hot food, a drink — all this blazed
from the hotel which stood fully lit in sheets of rain.

Laughter and cigarette smoke were spilling through open doors
and they could see couples dancing, women in strapless gowns,
men in full evening attire, the usual white-coated boys padding
to and fro with trays of drinks. What the hell? Are they idiots?
Matson voiced it for all of them.

They straggled into the lobby, kowtowed to by a doorman still in livery, and Charles felt acutely the drowned look of himself and his group. He headed for the desk and asked for Pilchard. Sorry, so sorry, all gone.

Well, they've packed it in, he told his men. Probably at Cilapcat by now. Right, let's get a drink. Clustered together, sticky with rain and uncivilized sweat, they decided the Dutch were busy using up their liquor supplies. Remarkable how a stiff gin, Dutch gin at that, and the fragrance of Player's, could make things seem almost normal. But as they watched this curious replay of the dances and charity balls in full swing when the coast of Malaya was breached months ago, Matson protested, they must know that Java's about to fall. . . ?

Civilians, Charles said. They've seen HQ pull out. Where would they go?

That bloody train . . . someone ventured. If they can't repair the line we'll be sitting ducks.

We'll have to slog it on foot.

They began to argue about the most expedient course: following the rail line where they would be visible, or striking out through the jungle. Hopeless without a guide. You can't trust the natives, they're all fifth column. And there was the question of time.

Charles stared at the waltzing figures. The whole thing was unreal, the music, the good liquor warming them, the absurd possibility of trekking out. He supposed they'd have to give it a go — who wanted to dance while waiting?

The band shifted into a melody that cut through him. ". . . the way you sip your tea . . ." He could almost smell her Chanel . . . "the way you smile and speak . . ."

He wavered into a void where drivenness, the sharp focus of will simply left. There were still the voices arguing back and forth, the clatter of glasses, a woman's thrill of laughter — but none of it touched him. How odd, a part of him thought, so this is what it will be like.

—

waiting in line for tenko to be over, the morning count, the noon count, standing in the noon sun without a hat waiting for the stupid guards to tally their individual counts — why can't they get it right? do they do it on purpose? but you can't say anything, you can't even look impatient or you might get your face slapped like the Dutch woman wearing lipstick. didn't she know it's an affront? or had she reached her limit? sometimes it happens waiting for tenko to end, having the trots, holding it in, praying you won't disgrace yourself — they're starting all over again, somebody's miscounted, they've forgotten the sick, your neighbour whispers. again. waiting for tenko to end and feeling the blurred edges of a faint — maybe it's standing for so long, maybe it's the coffee of burnt rice, maybe it's the abscess on your leg, maybe it's just the rice, rice porridge, rice loaf, rice rice, nice rice — waiting for tenko to end and wanting to scream. they're starting again — maybe it's how they shout their numbers, bullying with their short-legged strut, their tenko-tenko, prodding you into line, making you bow, hitting you because of how you look. no choice — don't think of that. think of the choir and singing Miss D's new hymn, Give us patience to endure, Keep our hearts serene and pure . . . then what? . . . think it again . . . and over again . . .

—

Sighs of relief as the train creaked into Cilapcat late in the afternoon. Just an overgrown fishing village really. Stepping down into the throng of people dragging baggage from the cars, desperate people who had somehow known to head this way, they moved through the crowd pushing its way to the quay.

Aside from the usual clutter of sampans and fishing junks, the only boat of any size was a rusty tramp steamer, the General Bass, one of those small supply boats routinely chugging up the coast with a carrying capacity of some dozen passengers. Charles spotted Pilchard on deck arguing with several Javanese crew. On the wharf below stood a knot of naval officers he recognized, some evidently on guard duty.

Just in time old man! It was Anderson, their counterpart at headquarters. Here's our escape tub.

We're making a run for it on that? Matson was dubious. Despite all the sailing he and Charles had done in Malaya, neither of them had ever seen naval duty on a ship, let alone under fire.

Pilchard, leaning forward from the railing, nodded curtly at their salute, How many men? Then turned immediately to Hopper who was lugging a sack of rice up the gangplank. That's all you could find? He's looking grim, Charles thought, he knows it isn't going to be easy.

We've rounded up a couple of sacks of rice, Sir, some local veg, nothing more. Should we use force?

No, Lieutenant.

Detailed to see about taking on fuel, Charles found himself at the end of the wharf by the oil tanks face to face with an obdurate Dutchman who, he said, could not possibly authorize the R.N. to take his supply without a permit. After wasted minutes, Charles went off to fetch Pilchard. He's going by the book, Sir.

To hell with that! Pilchard was young for a C.O. but he was the most senior officer there. He elbowed through the crowd milling about on the quay. A young Dutch woman with two children grabbed Charles' sleeve and spoke in heavily accented English, Please! please take us!

He gestured helplessly, It's not up to me, Madam. Sir? he called to Pilchard's retreating back — Pilchard, who was young and driven by time.

He threw a furious look at Charles. You know what's going to happen out there tonight, Lieutenant. We cannot possibly expose women and children to that sort of danger.

But, he wanted to argue, what will they be exposed to here? He knew what Pilchard would say — Where do we draw the line?

Maybe she knew it was hopeless, he thought as he mumbled something to the panic in her eyes.

Two steps ahead of him Pilchard was storming into the wharfinger's office. Look, in case you are unaware of the gravity of the situation, enemy forces will be occupying Cilapcat in a matter of hours. If we don't take that oil, they will.

You must show a permit. Stubborn, officious, the man stewed in his curved wooden chair, disliking the British, refusing to believe them.

This, Pilchard drew his revolver, is my permit.

—

was it having to spend a penny or do your job in front of everyone? was that what brought it home? that you would never be there again, not the home you knew when you hadn't even known what grown up meant? this lifting of skirts in front of everyone — the ladies you'd never imagined doing it, the matrons your mother taught you always to be polite to — curious eyes, glimpses of bodies in so many shapes, buttocks hanging fat or thin, wobbling thighs, and hair, so much hair down there —

you hadn't imagined that at the fancy dress party at the Club when you'd gone as a Spanish dancer, black lace on your hair and that wonderfully scarlet tiered dress your mother had made, and you'd worn lipstick and black mascara and tossed your head when they said how grown up you looked —

you hadn't imagined when you went with your mother to wash in the grimy water from the tong — you were among the last ones that night — and your mother said, now clean yourself down there, and you hadn't wanted the water to touch you — wash, she said, and you refusing when the guard walked in — his bayonet, his split-toed boots, and you stark naked. you felt her stiffen — he was looking you up and down with that look you'd seen on men looking at women, a look that meant something you'd only begun to imagine — was it then you knew you were old enough after all?

———

Standing with their backs against the cabin wall, peering into rain that had suddenly descended in sheets sprayed off the deck, he felt grateful — not just that they happened to be only half wet while others were still fumbling out there with the lifeboats on rusted davits. But braced against fear, the ship's pitch, it dawned on him that the explosion was not going to happen.

For long minutes now they had been waiting for the third strike, the one that would be dead on — I think we've lost them, he said to Matson, watching the next man turn with the same thought, a sudden tentative grin running from face to face.

Extraordinary! Matson almost groaned. It was extraordinary, Charles thought, fumbling for cigarettes and offering them, almost dropping the one he pulled for himself. His hands were shaking. And the wind kept blowing out his lighter so that they had to face in to the wall. Give us a turn, mate. They moved out from their dry spot, trying to keep that ordinary smoke going for as long as they could.

72

The ship was crowded to the gunwales with naval personnel and civilians desperate to get out (men only, Pilchard had insisted right up to the last). Assigned to forward watch while others had been put on cooking or sanitary crews, Charles stood next to Matson as they chugged out of Cilapcat, much too bright a moon illuminating the waters all around them. As they cleared land they could see the dark mass of Java loom behind, and above it, blackness, no stars.

Looks like we might lose that moon, Charles said as they watched the blackness boil and begin to gain on them.

Then the first call from the crow's nest: submarine track, starboard to port, forward. And immediately afterwards, the man astern: torpedo track, starboard to port, astern. Two ranging shots as the sub got a bead on their midships. The order came to stand fast, as people thronged to the lifeboats, but what was the point? Charles thought, backing up against the nearest wall. And then wild chaos descended, the blessed relief of a tropical storm.

Somehow the sub had lost them. Somewhere down there in relative calm while a torrent raged above. It didn't make sense. It did, there was that Hand again. He felt a sudden exhilaration as fear drained and waves smashed up around their tub of a boat taking them forward in their miraculous lives.

⎯ HOW I LOVE MORNINGS HERE — five first words written to connect with you. First words of the new month i was taught for luck in another country, hares and rabbits — rabbits anyway, squatting, ears alert, the runaway rabbits of North End Road perched very still in the mist. Echoes of childhood fabulae. I want to write you here, translate you, into this fabulous air so drenched with the syllables of birds. I want to pour you into this bowl of misty half-light, everything merged, submerged — our island dawn, just beginning . . .

I still write *our*, just as i long to write *you* without separation . . .

Just as family, the idea of family with its unbroken bond, haunts our connection. A thread of magic litanies running back, uncut, like Ariadne's to a safe place.

When my mother first learned this particular charm (to alter the destiny-freight a whole month might bring) she hadn't thought of me yet, could never have imagined you . . .

Breaking the marriage script, we broke the familial ties we each were meant to perpetuate. And yet, so many strands of the old scripts that compose us wove the narrative, then unreadable, unread, that made me recognize you when you walked into that crowded café. Rain clothes giving up their wet in the coffee-warm, people warm, you leaning passionate over cups and saucers to connect. We told each other intimate stories and i watched you grow clear, you i'd been waiting for, over the cognac we ordered — luminous threads from that farm in the Midwest, where you are now, flaring toward other threads from across the Pacific, about to catch light and spill their difference into each other . . .

Like milkweed pods, the way they split, webs of intermingled hair, seed, shining threads blowing along the gravel road . . .

There's a Midwest image for you, Lori. An island one too. All that milky juice staining our hands. Now you find you have to break more strands, the ones i thought we were weaving new from the old breakage. I felt them tearing as you spoke. Telling me in that decisive tone of yours that you have had enough of islanding.

A rock in my throat, that impossible thing. I couldn't speak, not on the phone. All i could think is that now we must untangle the different strands of our story.

———

After steaming off-course into the Indian Ocean, evasive action, their commandeered boat arrived in Fremantle, rationless and almost without water. He was sent on to Melbourne where he was claimed by the Australian Navy and posted to the "Cerberus, additional to Navy Office." What amounted to an office job in ciphers made life together possible and he cabled Esme at once. The city, he wrote, was full of people they knew. He would find them a flat, even a hospital if beds were to be had. Two months before her due date, she joined him.

Their child was born into a fragmented circle of refugee friends, Auntie this and Auntie that, and grandparents duly settled in a Melbourne hotel. This was, after all, an experience Aylene would not miss, though she declared herself unready for the role and abhorred its name.

You can't be too careful with names, she announced, peering into the minute face presented to her. Names shape destinies. Look at *Esme*.

Holding up her dark-haired progeny for inspection, Esme wondered what destiny her mother had attached to *Esme* twenty-four years ago. Whatever it was, the bundle of rosy flesh, blanket-wrapped and adorably present, seemed to justify her existence.

Sally she thought a perfect name: small and unaffected, nothing a child would have difficulty living up to. Aylene was scandalized. How could you dream of giving your daughter a darky's name?

That was the first battle, with Suzanne the finally agreed-on compromise. A Gallic twist to an unpretentious garden variety. For heaven's sake darling, don't, whatever you do, let people call her Suzie. You know what Australians are like — calling your father Vik. Vik! As if he were some Bombay taxi-driver.

Naming the grandparents proved equally difficult. I simply cannot abide Gran or Granny — unbearably common. It makes me feel as old as the hills.

Gradually, after months of gurgles at the heavily powdered face with its up-and-down melodics, indistinguishable baby sounds were seized with triumph and turned into Giggi, later contracted in writing to Gigi with a Parisian flair.

Gigi and Grandpa, so be it. Peace was more important than honesty, Esme told herself, though once, pinching her nose at the smell of the nappy bucket, she hurled accusations into the offending air: your life hasn't changed one jot, Mother, though the world has. Paris, with all its bistros and can-can, is occupied. Do you know what that means?

Apart from the name, this new role required certain props. An ornate walking stick, for instance, which had nothing to do with medical support. And so the two Babas, as Esme first tried calling them, each with their stylish canes, grew larger and larger as they approached from the nearest tram, he in his homburg, she in her turban with its jewelled pin. Always she carried a large handbag that held seductive sweets and other lures to distraction — used tram tickets, a glass swizzle stick (oh Mother, do be careful), two artificial violets, badly creased (just watch out she doesn't put them in her mouth).

(It's extraordinary, Charles said, your parents have no idea how to raise a child. How did they manage with you? They didn't, she replied. My ayah did.)

In this way the child, born in a would-be republic affirming its ties to the British throne, began her life with imperial words. No ayah but two babas who would relieve her hard-pressed mother on occasion. Baba, just a consonant shift off dada and mama. Could they escape hearing its Malay resonance from their Malacca and Penang days? Esme recalling with nostalgia her Nonya-Baba amah from a community generations-old speaking Hokkien- and English-sprinkled Malay, cooking dishes like curry capitan, shopping in sarong kebayas.

Baba grandfathers spent hours sipping kopi and exchanging chakap. Suzanne's grandfather liked his chakap too, preferably with retired medical cronies in hotel lounges. He lived in an English wool suit and punctuated tea with the routine reminiscence: a whiskey sucoh, now that would hit the spot.

Nevertheless he grew into Grandpa (to go with Gigi) of the coughing chuckle, the waistcoat that smelled of medicine and old cigar smoke, the silver watch that disappeared in a pocket. Grandpa cursed Churchill and loved him, just as he sometimes smacked her bottom, then played "dickey-bird" and slid her a toffee. Grandpa talked about India, talked about Malaya, taught her "Rule, Britannia," to sing it standing up like Little Grey Rabbit: "Britons nevah nevah nevah shall be slaves."

—

Oh Lori, this was never part of the story woven around you. A baby-boomer making your appearance in a demobilized USA busy sending war vets to college and working women back into the home, you inherited other clothing: Pollyanna dresses, yes, but also pint-sized dungarees, cowboy boots. You remember the plowed furrows stretching away from the house, shelves of preserves and your mother weeping in the basement. You remember Roy Rogers and your own pony in the barn. Angel food cake, chores with your brothers. A certain undertone at the dinnertable dissonant with words like "commies" and "unions."

So recently we stood in our own kitchen hushed, listening to the news. Darkness outside and ourselves figured in the window like apparitions on a TV screen. The sound of bombs, an excited journalist's voice describing the street from his hotel window. Baghdad blowing up. We were appalled for different reasons, historically accountable and furious at a complicity neither of us wanted to recognize.

But it is not this war that divides us, with its lines of punishment and revenge. It's something further back in our own lives. Still unread.

Their "Melbourne days," as Esme referred to them later, lurched on in beleaguered domesticity framed by news from Europe, news from the Pacific, which alternately offered them hope (in 1943 peace seemed just around the corner) or depressed them with defeats and still more death tolls. By 1944 war seemed a permanent condition of life.

Charles sent regular letters to his father, writing sometimes during quiet moments at night in the Navy Office, engaged in work he never described, though he mentioned long hours, 8 a.m. to 11:30 p.m. Nothing about the nature of his job, some general commentary on the progress of the war and concern for his father's own long hours as ARP Warden in southern Kent, well within reach of German rockets and bombs.

"Dear Dad," he begins the letter still encased in its almost square envelope, 3 *Opened by Censor* stamped in red ink down one end, "It is a wet depressing day & I have no letter from you to answer. The problem is what to write about. You probably face the same problem in writing to me. The usual daily round of life continues & its little interests seem so trifling against a background of world war that it seems futile to write of them . . ."

He comments on the crowds of Easter holidaymakers on the trams as he goes on and comes off duty each day of the long weekend, Anzac day extending free time, at least for civilians, into the week. "You would not think the maximum war effort were being made, as is so often proclaimed to the world, if you lived here." Luna Park is bright with arcade lights and music. Theatres are advertising Betty Grable in *Song of the Islands*, Lana Turner in *Slightly Dangerous*.

What does he think about at midnight as he tiptoes into the darkened bungalow, black shoes in hand, groping past kitchen chairs to the sink where he lets the tap run, breaking the noise of its fall by cupping his hand in its small torrent — waterfalls he has hiked to in Kedah? the Waterfall Road to the Botanical Gardens in Georgetown? The first grim news of POW camps in Malaya, atrocities in Burma? Clean water, clean and ordinary.

He is tired of what constantly leans in on them, the news from elsewhere, the good news, the bad news he can do nothing about, the wish for it all to be over, the worry about missing friends, a future, the old life that has fallen away when he felt he could make a difference, shape something of value.

Some nights there is no silence.

He arrives to find Suzanne fretting, fevered with yet another cold, Esme desperate for sleep. He takes the child into the parlour and settles down on the sofa, talking to her in words she doesn't understand, and when the crying starts again, rocking her small hot body in his arms as he lets his attention wander and the brain that is full of letters and numbers unwind in the dark, a spool of film cascading off its sprocket onto the floor.

—

He in his winter uniform, greatcoat wrapped around his legs, neatly creased trousers underneath. Seated on a park bench with a baby bundled in white on his lap, graphic in the disparity between the crisp lines of his naval cap, his dark uniform, and her round white form. Holding her awkwardly, firmly, as if she might slide from his grip, he has one shiny shoe upraised, caught in the jounce that will keep her smiling for the camera.

Toddler arranged on a blanket in wool leggings and jacket, only her mouth visible, her grin as she tips her father's naval cap over her face to hide in all that white dark.

Young mother in slacks leaning against a pillar the baby is perched on. Hair rolled above her face, right leg bent slightly against the pillar. Her pose is casual as she smiles, displaying the look of young women in coveralls handily filling the gap in shipyards and factories. The look of a modern mother freed from incessant contact through bottle-feeding and proud of keeping a regular regimen.

The place itself has disappeared into faded sepia, a flickering sequence of frames, of black-cornered stills, "snaps." To send home to England or keep in a family album. Images in which they saw themselves contemporary, fluent in the idiom of adverts, news photos, film images that surrounded them. Their own unspeakable dreams translated into this language. Ghostly.

—

Esme pushed the pram to local shops, queued up with her ration coupons, smiled at shopkeepers. Exuding young matronhood like musk, she garnered compliments on her daughter's mass of Shirley Temple curls. A poppet, they said, a pretty tyke — she heard *take* and marvelled at their vowels.

Saving string, scrounging cardboard boxes for food parcels home to the father-in-law she had never seen, she enclosed brief, cheerful notes and daubed the whole with crimson sealing wax. He would not be disappointed, she promised. He would love her when, at the end of the war, they would finally meet — his granddaughter she meant — constructing thus a niche for herself in a family to which she belonged in name only.

She was keenly aware of raising the initial grandchild on both sides and she met her new responsibility head-on. She would be an entirely different mother from Aylene, she promised herself, a mother who knew what mothering meant. After all, she was armed with information her mother never had. She had Doctor Spock. And the papers were always talking about elimination of germs and the requisite soap, "safe even for tiny tots."

In a wartime culture of experts, the domestic theatre had its share of bulletins, and Viktor offered his. At fifty-six he was forcibly retired but still on active duty within his family. Advice on inoculations, knock knees, and a mysterious assortment of rashes was duly imparted. An early stint in India as Emigration M.O. had acquainted him with various exotic diseases, but Suzanne's typical eighteen-month-old body offered little in the way of medical diversion.

Nevertheless, a careful mother knew that disaster lurked around any corner, that germs infected the commonest things, money being easily the worst offender. Clean hankies were essential in the portable kit that Esme's handbag became. Hankies for bandages around scraped knees, hankies with twisted corners for lifting soot out of an eye, cologne-steeped hankies bunched with a little spit (and lipstick) for grubby cheeks. Spit and polish in the presentation of toddlers: evidence of one's professional mothering.

—

Bushed is what people call the feel of being immersed in the dark of trees, sky indeterminate from fog, and deer the only company for too long. They want to get back to the mainland, mainstream, the main thing, feeling as if they've been side-tracked. Is that what you feel?

As i walk the dog along North Beach Road — the cedar bend, the one we like, reeks of spring and soon wild currant will dangle its shocking pink — the sea drowns island reefs and then recedes, only to wrap itself around again. Amorous intent. Insistent rhythm even abandoned orchards feel.

To live here is to be invaded by such rhythms. Not invaded perhaps, but seduced, pore by pore.

This isn't enough, you say. This is what sidetracks us from a sense of direction in our lives, this losing ourselves in the surge and toss. Islanded, as if marooned. You return to the fatal idea of islands cut off from the main. Cut off from a larger narrative that builds and builds . . . toward what end?

Where can we be if we aren't where we are, inside so many levels of connection? Rooms afloat on a sea of electronic impulses, while fires rage unchecked and oil slick on a different gulf drifts toward a herd of breeding sea cows soon to be forgotten, immaterial finally in the human struggle for dominance.

I can't seduce you any more, can't call you back, can't begin to say what loving is. This place permeated by old betrayals . . . this place where radiance shimmers daily . . . the call and response that birds are full of . . . Something urgent and feather light in the balance.

—

Slowly the news began to change. Allied efforts in the Pacific were surfacing into big print. By late April *The Age* reported STRIKE ON SUMATRA after British carriers successfully steamed across the Indian Ocean to launch Barracudas and American Dauntless Avengers in a sunrise attack: ". . . the beginning of the road back to Malaya and Singapore," the paper crowed.

once you thought you knew where you were on a hazy kind of inner map, now you know that what Sumatra meant, or Palembang if you had even heard of it, was nothing to what they mean now. and oddly enough, the map has faded further with each year as if the rest of the world had simply dropped away. sometimes you and your current "family," your kongsee as you call it, think back through the camps and moves but time is unreal. what you know is this camp now, your particular barrack, your own bali-bali where you sleep between B. and S., the "lav" below no more than a cement drain, the mud walkways, the padang in the middle with the cookhouse and guardhouse at either end. you know them by the steps you make, the effort they take. the half-mile walk to the hydrant where you go in the heat to carry water back in kerosene tins, balancing them on a bamboo pole on your bony shoulders like a coolie. you carry water for the garden, where the baked mud must be broken up with chungkals, their blades coming down in enforced unison in the sun. you are learning to know nothing beyond the camp, except the road just beyond the gates where you file out at five in the morning to clear grass with parangs, bending in the sickle rhythm as pre-dawn birds sing and the one stray dog that has not been killed comes sniffing round, almost as thin as you. and now that rice rations have been cut still further you are learning the jungle under the eyes of the guards, foraging for plants you never knew were edible, ferns, wild vines, dahlia-like leaves. you know where the graves are, patches of raw earth. you try not to think of this. you are thirsty all the time but there is only bad well water to drink, one Klim tinful per day. dust infiltrates your skin, dried-out dust from your own "manure" (the word BM, like modesty itself, belongs to another place), dust from the rain-flooded cesspools you've had to drain with coconut shells, singing the Captives' Hymn that M. has written, singing the words with all your heart so as not to smell the stench that invades your hair, your clothes, even the cracks in the hardened soles of your feet. but you don't smell this now or even see the sores on lips and legs, the ribby chests as you sing along

87

with the others. you hear M's voice soliciting, encouraging yours, you see Sister C's bare legs scrambling up the atap roof to patch it in a storm, you hear B's coughing chuckle as she invents another extravagant recipe to dream over. so you stand there singing and your heart swells to hold this ragtag retinue lost somewhere in a mapless world.

—

Civilian life in Melbourne chugged on, despite grass fires and calls for extra labour at harvest-time (teachers on summer vacation pitched in at the jam factories). Mundane hours in St. Kilda were punctuated by the grandparents' coming and going. Over tea one afternoon, Aylene claimed that she missed cooking, living as they did on other people's notions of a decent meal. Shortages in England, Charles' concern about his widowed father's cooking, the availability of dried fruit and even butter with more generous Australian rations, all gave impetus to the dramatic production of fruitcakes — Aylene's contribution to the war effort.

The ritual began with a very big bowl in the middle of the kitchen table. While Esme hovered, bringing ingredients from various cupboards, Aylene gave orders from memory: a teacup of this, a dessertspoon of that. Suzanne watched the spoon turn more and more slowly as the candied peel, and then the sultanas and nuts were folded in with precious marmalade to keep the cake moist on its long sea-voyage. Allowed to kneel on a chair on the other side of her grandmother's elbow, Suzanne leaned close to the warm bulk of her beige cardigan, the heavy arms with their sleeves rolled up (Suzanne's own sleeves were rolled up too — so we can both get dirty, dear), the scarf-ties of her blouse tucked up behind Esme's apron (transformed Gigi, somehow more comfy as she groaned, as she grunted — oh poor Gigi — as the two jewelled hands and the two tiny hands pulled and pulled on the spoon which stood straight up). In between turns, Suzanne dipped her fingers one by one, scooping up dabs of it sticky-sweet and climbing, somehow, up her forearms, across her face (Mother, if you let her eat any more she'll have the collywobbles tonight), spoon and batter turning, turning until the triumphant propping sideways of the bowl (it took all three of them), the mixture pushed and prodded to a reluctant slide and then a large plop into paper-lined tins.

Collywobbles were beside the point. Anyway she wouldn't get them. Her Gigi, collapsed in the armchair, brushing wisps of hair away from her temples with the back of her wrist, and blowing out air — so that's done — her Gigi knew. Esme did the washing up.

—

By mid-June of 1944 winter as usual is upon them — cold, wet, dreary. He writes to his father:

"The report on the food outlook for Britain interested me very much. It is rather gloomy to think that there will be no improvement in the food available for you until 1947 — and that 1950 is the year held out as the earliest return to the pre-war standard. But perhaps events will move faster than the food experts think possible. The restriction on the quantity of cake that can be sent home has been reduced & one can now send up to 5 lbs . . . . we have sealed up about 4 lbs in a tin which is being dispatched to you."

They would have been sitting near the tiny fire in woollen dressing gowns over their clothes to keep warm, he in the armchair with a book against his knee to support the letter he was writing. On the sofa she pushed the newspaper aside with an impatient gesture. Enough of flying bombs or aerial torpedoes, whatever they wanted to call those things raining down on southern England. Hitler's "reprisal weapon No. 1." Even the cinema page — Fred Astaire and *The Sky's the Limit* — only exhibited the boundless optimism and nerve of the Yanks. Could they really win the war?

The adverts made her realize that she and Charles hadn't been out to a flick in months. He was so often working at night. And now that he was here, all he wanted to do was write a letter. Curled up with a cup of tea going cold beside her, she watched his precise hand covering the page with its tiny script. She was truly sick of the war, the way it infiltrated their life, draining any sort of pleasure. This endless making-do, their real lives on hold, this waiting for it all to end. Yet who was she to complain? she with her husband safe and a home for their child. Even if they did have a landlady who was trying to turf them out so she could charge a higher rent to some non-Service family. Typical Aussie opportunism. No, they would never fit in here. They were only birds of passage, nesting temporarily on some rocky islet. Compared to Dorothy and so many other wives who could only wait for inevitably awful news, she was lucky.

He had stopped writing for a moment and was gazing into the fire with that sober, reflective look that was almost severe. Watching him covertly, she realized she had no idea what he was thinking. Was he getting bored, losing interest in her?

She glanced down at the paper again. Two young girls pert in Red Cross uniforms, their bloom slightly unreal. Everything had changed and nothing had changed. The mean ordinariness of life, that Eno's ad staring up at her, GOOD HEALTH IS YOUR FIRST DUTY SO USE YOUR ENO'S SPARINGLY, OUR TROOPS IN THE

TROPICS NEED IT — bowel movements and the war effort (why should they need Eno's more frequently in the tropics anyway?). Australian crassness. And the way the government had rationed meat and then run ads promoting bread, BREAD TO THE RESCUE, all those proteins and vitamins, they said, and something called gluten, which was a "meat-equivalent," when everyone knew bread couldn't replace meat for growing children. The war was everywhere and everyone was obsessed with it.

He had gone back to his letter. No doubt he was a much better son than she was a daughter — odd, considering the rather formal tone of his letters. Or perhaps not so odd, perhaps nearness kept all the old irritations alive. She was getting tired of her father's incessant Kipling. As the war dragged on he seemed to be growing more and more remote. It's only because he has no useful work, dear. Yes, Mother, I know. But he was hanging onto something that was already outmoded. All those gallant ideas, the bravery, the flag waving — *You're a better man than I am, Gunga Din!* When would he have said that to any of his servants?

But then war was all about the comradeship men felt fighting side by side, risking their lives for each other. Their deaths had meaning, were written up in newspaper accounts, memorialized in poems.

And what of the deaths that weren't? The prisoners who were dying inch by inch, refused water like those soldiers in Burma, or forced to labour on sweltering roads with no food. What about the hacked-up bodies of those women in the French doctor's wardrobe in Paris, and all the disjointed bones. Thirty different pairs of shoes they'd found. Thirty-four bodies they thought, though it was hard to tell after the lime had done its work. Her mind kept returning to this. *Paris is a city of hunger, lawlessness and fake gaiety*, the paper said, as if to explain that that was what occupation did, and why men fought against it. But why women, why was it always women whose bodies were found this way? And who were they? What lives had they been living that were stopped so abruptly — new shoes perhaps, one of them proud of her new shoes that very day. It was never they who were remembered, only their murderers. Dr. Petiot, Dr. Landru. Jack the Ripper. With or without war.

—

Nights are the worst — i never dreamt that nights could be so bright. The image of a greased cormorant struggling to lift itself from oil-thick waters in the Gulf of Bahrain repeats and repeats. Irreversibly awake i drag a chair to the window overlooking the lake and sit in a halo of light radiating off the moon's track. You've left without saying goodbye, without even looking back, and i am left in unthinkable space. How could the dialogue of our eyes, that deep and ecstatic look we held each other by, reading the dark places as well as the radiant ones, how could the tenderness that soaked our skin have come to this?

I can't think of anything to write, to say, that will alter your direction. Your speech so closed, impatient, when I called to ask what you meant — "I have to figure out my life. Can't you see?" I see the moon-track swings slowly, slowly, and only one way.

—

His letters home were full of domestic news, perhaps the only news that would safely pass the censor. He was conscientious about security. Or did that near escape off the coast of Java fuel a new pleasure in home, in the child he would otherwise have missed?

92

There is news of a second baby on the way. "This is the result of a lot of careful consideration . . ." He lists three reasons in point form, a) wanting to have two children and fearing that if they wait he and Esme may be separated again — he will have to return to Malaya, and postwar conditions might necessitate her staying in Australia for some time; b) their daughter, "such a source of joy and interest . . . runs the danger of becoming a spoilt only child"; c) as for expense, the war news is now so encouraging that "by this time next year I may well be out of the Navy and in some more lucrative occupation."

Punctilious logic, inculcated in British schools, to justify an additional responsibility his father might view as unnecessary? Despite his rational façade, he is nursing dreams. Events have beached him on a shore where he is temporarily cooling his heels. He would make the most of this time, with its confined perspective. But already he dreams beyond it, planning his release, planning how he might get to work in the rubble of Malaya rebuilding the company, the country. The dream of continuity. Could he glimpse then the end of the Empire and the beginning of a new order? Chinese towkays and Malay officials in uneasy liaison against the British. Believing in the country against his own interests, he would find these political crosscurrents engaging.

And she? Every other letter he writes home contains the promise of one from her, if she can find the time, he adds. By the end of the war they will have two small children and a third on the way. She already has her hands full.

—

Suzanne was swinging on the Caulfield gate. It was time for tea, but tea wouldn't really begin until her Babas came. She had been

93

waiting a long time, jiggling the gate in its lock, running back to the house (Esme busy putting the tray together, exasperated that they were late as usual), running back and jumping up on the gate again (just keep looking, darling, and don't come back til you see them), fitting her feet in their brown boots between the bars of the gate, wishing it would open so she could really swing, as she did when Grandpa pushed her, his hand firmly against her bottom, again and again with that satisfying bang — What a racket! Viktor, must you?

The child's a little minx, he would protest, as if it were her fault. Then as they trooped into the house and she hovered beside him, he would wink from under his bushy brow — Aren't you, pal-o-mine-o?

—

Successive news of the retaking of the Marshalls, the Admiralty Islands, and then the Mariannas meant that they could believe the Americans had indeed turned the tide. "Mopping up" became the metaphor and civilian life moved closer to the front page. Melbourne celebrated American Independence Day. There was talk of air travel replacing sea voyages and of international telephone connections bringing New York as close as Geelong. Planned kitchens were the thing. Pedometers attached to the heels of British housewives revealed that they walked five miles in an average day ("No wonder I'm exhausted," Esme sighed). The three hundred steps a woman took to bake a cake ("three *hundred*, Mother!") could be cut to forty-eight.

Aylene tossed this aside, much to Esme's irritation. But darling, if you have a houseful of servants, and you will when you go back, what difference does it make?

Oh, Esme thought, she's regretting Dad's retirement. No salary, no servants, a poky little flat somewhere in England, all those bombed-out streets. Suddenly she felt as if she and Charles had their lives before them. They would return to Penang on a full tide.

At the beginning of the Melbourne album full of baby photos, grandparents and babies, Mummy or Daddy with babies, there is a single photo of her that must have been taken before the war, before the children. She stands alone on a black page above silver capitals — *storage pocket for prints and negatives* — wearing a huge sunhat that frames her face. White sashes end in a floppy bow under her chin. Beneath the demure golfing skirt her calves bow backwards because she is schoolgirl straight in her white socks and dark shoes, standing up to a chest-high dahlia, one hand out to it, face turned full to the camera and tipped slightly — heavy-lidded eyes, darkly coloured lips. This girlish pose, almost theatrical, this smile hiding expectancy under a look of determined effervescence — Whatever she is offering (sunhat or dahlia head) has yet to be assessed. And the dahlia gleams (yellow?) white in the black and white, so bright all detail is lost.

Near the close of '44, when she has begun to "show," she will disappear from his cine footage. The camera veering away from the back she turns, her irritated hand flailing at it.

—

What is this urge to fix an image so it won't fade over time? Positives preserved in all their purity as if to evidence what we actually experience — quicksilver, transient.

So i wake at dawn not sure whether this variegated trilling, pure liquid delight, is only a dream of my childhood place — wet n, wet rockface, the cave i wanted to crawl into and wasn't owed, the endless litany of dawn with its beckoning to live, come out, come outside of the house and live . . . the dream i wanted to dream you into . . .

In the luxury of stretching out, my body skips the present to seek yours, seek your warmth with all pores open. Then i remember you are not here and it is the gulf between us that is stretching wide, so difficult to cross.

I am on this side of it, preoccupied with memory, taken with illuminant desire, that white beam flashing its images. Hallucinatory.

Video flicker. Peripheral passage last night. Migratory birds flying, whole flocks across the oil-slick in that other contested Gulf. Driven by homing desire past fire, through impenetrable smoke. While below them the bombing and the firing go on.

What is this desire to occupy or else destroy?

I want to rage at it. Child rage. Even as i dream you, desire that bliss of total surrender, bliss at the dissolution of blockage — old wounds, the ones we tell over and over as if they were our selves. "You" escape, you other than my dreaming designs. I forget (are we always complicit?) that dreams are drawn to the blurred ideal each of us carries — home, the impossible place, love, the mother our own mothers, amid the urgent particulars of their lives, could never live up to.

—

In her Form 5a prize, Palgrave's *Golden Treasury* with its gilt print on brown leather, the school's initials emblazoned on a shield over *Carpe Diem*, she underlined in neatly ruled pencil:

I can give not what men call love;
But wilt thou accept not
The worship the heart lifts above
And the Heavens reject not:
The desire of the moth for the star . . .

Drawn to Shelley's otherworldliness in the long deprivation school was. Already desiring what was out of reach.

Charles was twelve years older when she met him, and on his way to becoming an old Malaya hand, revelling in the job that took him through mountain passes to company estates near Kroh, or southward to the tin mines of Taiping and Ipoh. Auburn-haired emissary dashing off with his syce in a green Fiat. She the dull brown moth? No, silver-winged and flecked with sorrow. Coloured by the lyric in its long astral reach.

Despite his precision with accounts, all those tiny figures stacked in columns, Charles had stories to tell of haunting and spirit-tapping. He was fascinated with Thaipusam and its religiously inspired transcendence of pain, the plunging of arms into hot coconut oil without a burn. He knew about the power of certain krisses that once belonged to warriors or Sultans — just stabbing a man's footprints would ensure his death. But these were stories told in a bemused tone and often with the word "extraordinary" attached. They leaked out at night in company, a dark vein under the skin of the day's logic he wanted his children to inherit.

He got Suzanne interested in stamp-collecting by bringing home small heaps of paper torn from envelopes at the office. Sitting her down at the dining room table he showed her how to soak them in curry tiffin fingerbowls and, while they were soaking, to peel apart the transparent hinges that stuck together

97

in their tin. Among others, the pages marked *Straits Settlements* — *Malaya* began to fill with colour. He insisted she learn the states: Perlis, Kedah (that mountain you can see from the swimming club), Perak (that's where Butterworth is, where the ferry goes), Kelantan, down the peninsula, Negri Sembilan, Malacca (where your mother used to live), Johore and all the way down to Singapore. So she would know where she lived, what she was (always with reservations) part of.

—

So i would know where i lived, what the birds were called, those bright bits of plumage on stamps, what the flowers were that flared on our table. To touch beyond the window the very texture of the place, soak in its smells, its sounds. This happened without question. What was questionable was the inner geography of home. The globe he bought for my birthday sat on the windowsill of the small room i graduated to, my own, just outside the bathroom. At night i heard their feet tiptoe past my bed, the quiet closing of the door, rushing sounds of water, and amidst it all their muted whispers. In the anteroom of their intimate life and half asleep i would strain to hear the words they spoke. Often the exciting smell of cigarette smoke and perfume trailed past and then i knew my mother had been out in his world, the world he fractured into names on the globe: Great Britain where King George lived, and the pinker territories of what had been her (this was confusing, why not his?) Empire: Canada with its seal fur, South Africa with its diamonds, India with its tea plantations . . .

The connections between. Trade and royalty. Armies and trade. Britannia standing over her turbulent waves as if nothing had changed. King George — *he* was King George (even our dog was royally named) and *she* was Britannia ruling a turbulent household. I knew he was King because she referred my questions about the world to him. But inside the world of our house and garden, her word held sway.

Shopping trips were the exception. Then i learned her version of empire as we went from stall to stall in the cloth bazaar while she talked barter-talk with the lean bearded men, fingering a length of this, a yard of that, denying, protesting in the face of their extravagant courtesy. But Mem, this price only for you. I was to learn patience, learn to respond politely when offered chai. I dragged my feet, dying to go to the cinema and watch Moira Shearer whirl her way through the graveyard in those extravagant red shoes.

Afterwards, Syce drove us home surrounded by brown-wrapped parcels of batik, of sharkskin, of Chinese brocaded silk, which she would unwrap and spread on her bed, exulting over the bargain she had driven for this one, regretting, with that one, his shrewdness and her inability to walk away.

Still, it was worth it, don't you think? she would appeal, holding it against herself in the mirror. Transformation and its charm. How could she, how could Karen in the film, *not* be taken with those Moroccan shoes of red leather?

—

Ghosts. Each of us already haunted. When i told you about the pretas, those black holes of never-satisfied desire that pursue us, your face clouded over. Do you really believe in such things? you asked, thinking how superstitious. All this talk of ghosts. We know about women's desire, we know the material conditions that must be changed to satisfy it.

The immaterial and how to deal with it materially. You liked the story our friends told of the ghost who sent crockery spinning off the shelf, knocked a floor lamp onto the bed — And that was when we were *in* it, Mika said, so we'd had enough. We told her, look, we don't mind sharing space, but if you're going to hang around you'd better make yourself useful and fix the washing machine. She disappeared.

You looked at me and i knew what you were thinking. Could my ghosts fix the washing machine?

—

His letters bore the simple return address c/o Navy Office, Melbourne — no street, simply a place he disappeared to. As soon as Suzanne was old enough, Esme began taking her into the City (never downtown — that was later, that was Canadian, and the City was a holdover from London), going by tram to the dark and crowded streets, Big and Little Collins, arcades with their illuminated windows, hundreds of feet clattering in heels, Myers' Emporium where, under the money pinging in wooden bobbins over their heads, Esme picked things up and regretfully put them down again. Or to Lyons' tea-shop to meet Dorothy or Wyn and, if there was time, if it wasn't raining, if Wyn's three boys squirmed too much or dropped their spoons, to the leaf-spattered pond in Treasury Gardens where they could chase ducks and scare up pigeons, as long as they didn't go near the trench shelters.

Their fur coats falling open, handbags beside them, the women sat on a bench and talked in low voices. They dressed up for each other, determined to look stylish in this brief respite from kitchen and typewriter. Dorothy was the only one who would glance at her watch, but she was also the one who spoke most seriously. Perhaps it was because she was different, Suzanne thought, she was a godmother.

Whenever Suzanne got tired of tagging after the boys, she would wander back and lean against her mother's knee, lulled by their voices and an occasional absentminded caress. Letting the trampled grass drift in and out of focus through the weave of their words, she half-listened to the names that preoccupied them: Changi, Burma, Geneva Code, dysentery. She didn't know these names and even some of the words she knew sounded different in their talk: starving (you must be *starving*, her Gigi would say after a long walk). No Red Cross, no medical aid, no doctors — what about Grandpa?

When she said it, her mother kissed her very slowly on the forehead. You don't know, darling, how lucky we are.

—

Responding to April and May letters from his father in Kent, letters which had arrived months later, he writes:

"The Government at home seems to have been more successful in dealing with the coal problem than our people here have been. We still have our strikes though not so many of them lately. Yesterday a collier came in and provided coal that averted a gas stoppage — the Gas Co. were down to their last day's stocks. So far, we have not had the supply cut off but we seem to live on very much a hand to mouth basis.

"I am glad that the parcel turned up at a propitious time and in good condition. I really must get down to sending you another one. It is deplorable, the way the weeks go by with so little accomplished. Our intentions are always so good, but it is difficult to carry them into effect."

The real news, the news he knew but could never communicate, shut up inside his head, he writes only of what is outward —

scarcities of daily life, uncles dying at home, the weather, always the weather.

This creates a curious vacuum, displaced as they are, and dependent on others fighting for their future. So he writes of the terrible cold, icy winds driving down off the mountain ranges to the north of them where once, not so long ago, they had revelled with friends. Meagre fire, meagre stories, meagre spirits. Repeated letdown after repeated hope. "As luck would have it," "if the tide continues to turn in our favour," the common currency of his letters.

—

Luck, fate, destiny rippled through Aylene's speech. Even D.V. was only a charm attached to the ends of her sentences. Attendance at Church on Sundays, though regular, was simply circumspect, part of one's social ticket, like proper dress. In Penang and Malacca it was followed by drinks and curry tiffin. And despite their sense of a mission, secular as it was, and jokes about native superstition, Viktor and those of his friends who counted themselves men of science would still be drawn at the end of an evening to Aylene's Ouija table.

This was when Esme felt her mother step into another realm, oracular, something beyond the social role she played so well. Aylene would order the lights to be turned low, except for one closest to the table. Its mahogany surface floated their faces inside a ring of letters, torn pieces of paper white as petals, their faces apparitional in a gauze of cigarette smoke. Doorways to the humming dark stood open, drumming somewhere far off, the Boy moving quietly with his tray of fresh drinks. What Esme remembered was the smell of smoke mixed with apprehension when their laughter died out.

That last night her eyes were fixed on the scarlet outline of someone's lips on a half-empty glass standing in its own little pool of sweat. The glass that was empty and upturned, the one she had her fingers on, almost touching her mother's perfectly lacquered nails, skimmed without their help in a wiry current of its own across the tabletop. Their contact identified himself as Ian, a civil engineer who had sat at their table only three months earlier. That was when Aylene's fingers had raced at the glass's bidding to spell out the word dam, the word Kedah. Now Ian was dead, buried in a mudslide when the dam he was inspecting had given way. Esme had flirted with him occasionally at dinner parties, and he had once told her that she was as delicate as Chinese porcelain. Now he was warning them, through the words, insane, foreign, end, and when her mother asked who? who? the glass began to spell out Esme.

Oh my dear, her mother whispered looking up, eyes lavender in the light. Viktor slammed his hand down. Enough! It's a stupid game. His friends rushed to fill the void with noises of agreement, and in the hubbub that followed, the women's soothing words, the Boy picking up pieces of glass, Esme caught a note. It was what they would take away to talk about, her mother's familiarity with spirits which had become something more than a parlour game. Her own daughter! the shocked and unspoken phrase. This Esme kept to herself, in the same recess where she hid the spelled-out words.

—

But she's not a ghost, you said once. She's in photos, on film, in letters. You have all these mementos you carry around with every move.

Yes, but — *mementos* was not a word i would have chosen for the evidence i felt compelled to keep. The lake was mirroring back the trees of the ridge, the lawn of the farm across the way. Maybe ghosts have something to do with presence and absence, both.

But how is that different from memory? you persisted. We both stared at the lake. Green surface on green depth. Glimmering. And everywhere micro-factories of light combining photo-chemical cells, radiant background to our words, our will to challenge each other.

Blind spots, i said. Maybe ghosts have something to do with our blind spots.

And i couldn't have guessed then how spring might happen this year. The end of February, and it wasn't the end of war, it was only a cease-fire, or so the headlines proclaimed. A cease-fire in darkness. Black fog, black pall over a newly liberated Kuwait. Moonless night. Six hundred oil wells ablaze by Hussein's last order. Headlamps of convoy trucks, lights burning in one or two hospitals, "killed" Iraqi-tank silhouettes on city streets. "This air we're breathing is full of oil."

"The cost of war," the paper summarized today in a colour-outlined box: an estimated 85,000 to 100,000 Iraqi troops killed or wounded. The unthinkable capabilities of the weapons that were used, never mind the weapons that weren't. And the enduring costs?

I wonder what you are feeling now amid the news on your side of the border. Perhaps our lives will carry on, perhaps we can reach out and cover over the blind spot . . . safe (apparently) from food shortages, stark grief, battered streets. We won't know how we were changed by it. This "Mother of Battles."

Strange how the heart fails, doesn't want to remember, tiptoeing around the absence a bed represents — her body in the soft abandonment of child-sleep. Eyes that would never open in all their amused or furious expressiveness. Heart attack in her sleep, the doctor said. The doctor i didn't want to call, wanting instead to go on sitting with her, refusing to let her body become a thing. That impossible sense of stoppage: she couldn't be gone, not without a word, not without a chance to say all that couldn't be said. Like children, Margo and i went through the bottles in her bedside table, looking for clues.

Their room, which was really hers, had always been off-limits except by invitation. The dressing table a laboratory with its crystal decanters, its silver-lidded powder bowl, its lustrous blue-backed brushes.

Teaching me the ritual hundred strokes, hair snagging in the bristles so my neck snapped each time she broke a knot, You don't know how lucky you are, she said, a woman's head of hair is her crowning glory. Her crowning glory, and her face her fortune, i mimicked back, not sure they were worth the trouble.

Younger and lying in her bed in the house up the hill, lounging in it sick but gratified to be playing with the new pastels she had bought in Singapore, i tried to draw her — mostly hair and colour, wonderful colours you could blur with a finger, magenta, chartreuse, rainbow dust all over my skin and the sheet (now she would be angry and now i couldn't show her . . .).

Too listless to do more than gaze in the heat at their wedding photo, i remembered what my father had said, how lovely she looked. So slim, so pale except for her lips. All that white cloth pooling and rippling at her feet. The tiny hat that looked about to slip off was holding down a veil that puffed like a cloud and then trailed around her. Her lips, dark and pouty-looking, were closed. With her arm tucked in his, he was grinning, about to make a joke to all those people. It looked like a party, someone holding a glass, Grandpa holding a cigar. Grandpa was the one who had given her away, she said. If it was a party it must have been a party for her — but why did she look so solemn? Sliding lower in the bed, rooting with my toes for luxurious cool at the end of the sheets, i was sure i would never let them give me away.

—

By late September he is commiserating in letters home to his father about the effects of flying bombs. "Now that details of the damage done have been released (over 1 million houses destroyed) we can begin to realize what a tremendous battering you in the South of England have been taking. Thank goodness, it now looks as if it is all over."

Three weeks later he notes angrily, "flying bombs are still being sent over England. I thought that when we had taken Northern France and Belgium, that peril would have passed."

Against this up and down graph line of war, his domestic bulletins continue. Reports of snapshots he is sending of Suzanne, and news of a lucky coup, some colour cine film for the Kodak he bought. Reports of food parcels with more of Aylene's cake on its way. Comments on his father's struggle with thieving rabbits in his vegetable garden.

"The war news is not so good," he writes, "swinging from recent over-optimism, the newspapers now indulge in over-pessimism and forecast several more years of war. I think this is wrong but perhaps that is wishful thinking on my part. In any case, I am very tired of the whole business."

More he cannot say, so he shifts to the domestic again. "Now that Esme is in the later stages of her second pregnancy, her mother comes over often to help with Suzanne and the cooking." He himself took much of his week's leave to spring-clean the house. Surprising how dirty a house can get when you can't keep up the cleaning.

—

All of them were used to having servants, including Aylene, born in India, a doctor's daughter. Scots-Irish, she always insisted, good blood. When she died in England just before her ninetieth birthday, they remarked how tiny she looked in the coffin, skin like a venerable Chinese lady, no white face powder to cover it. This echoed the story Esme told of holding new-born Suzanne, fascinated with her black hair, thick black lashes against the sleeping cheek — doesn't she look like a Chinese baby, Mother? Utter drivel, Aylene had snapped, how can you say such a thing about your own child?

Chinese? Indian? Eurasian women were noted for their beauty, even if they were déclassé. These stories, these colonial stories that perpetuate a making-strange — was it that they had spent so long, three generations born in the East, that they themselves began to feel un-English? Or was it that they were, and it was easier to make a life, to pass as English, if you erased the mixed part?

Records are sparse, the family stories stop with Aylene and Viktor. No image of who preceded them — except for an exotic great-grandfather visiting his patients by elephant and, on the other side, a policeman in Madras. Who were the women?

In any case, power remained in the hands of the Doctor, the Sahib, the Tuan. The children may have been born in the East, but they were packed off to school in England (for their own good), and perhaps his wife preferred it, didn't miss them with a busy social life and her husband's status to maintain. Yet once, near the end of her years, Aylene described their Melbourne days — all those babies — as the highlight of her life.

For Viktor the highlight was what had gone before, the British Empire, now tragically besieged. Quoting Kipling or Tennyson in grieved tones — *Break, break, break,/ At the foot of thy crags, O Sea!* — he raged against the Japs, lived heroism secondhand through newscasts, extolled the grandeur of man's struggle against evil. When he was in this mood, Charles found him bombastic, Aylene and Esme talked about cooking or the children. He's missing Penang, Aylene would sigh, and Esme understood what she meant — the clubbiness of that life centered on the hospital with its complex internal dramas.

He was always the doctor, Margo declared years later as we reminisced over plates of mah-mee. Did you know he saved Gigi's life? Her off-hand tone combined with melodramatic phrasing signalled a story about to be told. The family voice.

You mean in London? i threw in, not wanting to be outdone.

I don't know *where* — wherever it was she had pneumonia. The specialists had given up on her, you know, but Grandpa refused to let her die. He sat up with her day and night and wrapped her body in fresh wet sheets until he'd forced down the fever.

Now that was love, she sighed as we got up to leave the trendy Hong Kong noodle house in Vancouver's once-geriatric Chinatown.

That was sheer will, i revised, the will-power of a doctor and a colonial one at that.

—

Perhaps i haven't given you enough space, i think, my hands in the earth sprinkling tiny lettuce seeds that, once covered, will begin to sprout in the damp weather. I try to separate the tiny flecks of dormant energy, raking them with my finger to give each one enough growing room. Already i can imagine green rosettes appearing, the struggle with slugs, and then, if we're lucky, the pleasure of pulling leaves unfurled and crisp for the salads you love.

Perhaps i've been too absorbed with the past. If we can only talk about what you need — if you could just tell me — then we could make the necessary changes. (Even if that means leaving here? a little voice asks.) I push the wet soil into the shallow trench thinking of death again, of burned bodies in desert sand. (Perhaps we don't deserve this place, the little voice continues.)

Perhaps thinking *that* is the problem, i counter. Perhaps we don't understand where we really are.

—

Having no one else to play with in their garden surrounded by jungle, Suzanne and Margo played hospital, coaxing baby Lucy (she was always the baby, even when she could talk as well as they did) into playing the patient. When Lucy protested, they put their dolls to bed in shoeboxes in imaginary wards. Leaning over them solicitously, they took temperatures with sticks in odd places, bandaged arms and heads, and, warning them to be good, dosed them with brightly tinted medicines. Whoever was doctor bossed the nurses around, wrote importantly on scraps of paper, wrote prescriptions with invented symbols and unreadable words. For the mystic heart of this game was the dispensary: all those odd bottles lined up on makeshift shelves, the more curiously shaped the better, bottles saved from unknown uses just for playing hospital (o the sacred aura of medicine) shining blue, red, yellow in the sun — water dyed with colours Esme magically provided (blueing, cochineal, iodine) so long as they gave their word they would never drink it. In the name of medicine then, they dripped poison in their sick dolls' mouths, or in their ears, or in their eyes, stroked their foreheads, declared they would be better tomorrow. Went off and left them dosed up, left them lying there for hours.

———

Dorothy, have you seen *The Age*? Esme shouted into the telephone receiver. The operator had taken ages to ring through and Suzanne was whinging at her, tired of waiting in the cramped stuffy kiosk. If she opened the door the traffic noise would be unbearable. Still, if it was a choice between that and the whinging . . . With the reins of the harness wrapped around her wrist, she pushed the door ajar. Dorothy's voice sounded distant in all the hum. Why? What is it?

Listen. Propping her folded newspaper between the wall and her stomach, she read: *An offer to allow prisoners of war and interned civilians to cable home has been received by the British Government from Japan . . . All prisoners in Japanese hands would be allowed to send one 10-word cablegram, exclusive of address and signature . . .* That means you could be hearing from Brian!

Suzanne was pulling at the door. She pulled back, feeling her patience stretch to its limit.

There was a pause on the other end, then: Well, it will probably take weeks.

No, no. It's by *air*. They say: *the authorities have undertaken to forward messages from that area* — they're talking about *occupied territories* here so that must include Singapore — *as soon as possible by air mail.* She put her foot behind the section of door Suzanne was pushing.

How do we know we can trust the Japs to forward *anything*?

But it's through the Red Cross . . .

And anyway, I don't like the sound of that *would*. Why don't they say all prisoners WILL be allowed?

Oh Dorothy, it's *possible!* Esme urged. Suzanne had wriggled halfway through the door and was stuck, wailing loudly in protest.

You sound as if you have your hands full. Thanks so much for calling, my dear — and Dorothy rang off.

Why did I bother? Esme thought as she marched her spanked and sobbing daughter through the park. Had Dorothy fallen for someone else? Such things did happen. But no, Dorothy wasn't like that. And then she mentally kicked herself. Of course. Those reports of the wretched condition of POWs — hope was the worst thing.

—

It was this question — who was it who had preceded them? (into that otherwhere that ghosts and dreams come from) — that became material. Not elsewhere so much as an other here, less tangibly, less relentlessly present perhaps. But still present.

Esme had become mater, like her mother, and the old boarding school irreverence had fallen away. She had become solid, stamped with public approval. Like other mothers, she held the future of the nation in her hands — or so the government said, though it was hardly her nation. This was the same Esme who worried about being a good mother even as, her arms full of nappies taken from the line, fresh-smelling in a Melbourne wind, she could marvel at what she knew how to do. This pinning, this washing of tiny flesh, this learning of bedtime songs to sing, this spooning and making a game of it, this endless naming. Who was being trained? she sometimes wondered, yet at the same time exulted in clearing the hurdles. She knew this was what she had been saved for, shaped for, this redemption of her own childhood.

What her mother couldn't remember, the nurses had taught her, or friends with children passed on to her, even if it was unstated, picked up from covertly watching how they behaved with their own children. Viktor could always provide a medical solution: castor oil for constipation, calamine for rashes. Sometimes she took his advice, sometimes she filed it away for future emergencies. Children were so fragile, so unprotected finally, and he was hardly a pediatrician. Yet he *was* the doctor, a doctor who had said she would never have made a good nurse.

There were days when she longed for something she knew she couldn't expect: a sure knowledge, an easy familiarity with mothering Aylene might have passed on — like mother's milk, she thought, and then recoiled. It was impossible to imagine her mother, who worried about babies spitting up on her and complained of grubby little hands, it was difficult to imagine Aylene ever nursing a baby. Amazed that she had never wondered until now how she had been nursed, she realized she must have been handed over to a wet-nurse, an ayah hired so that her mother could carry on her social round. Who had that first ayah been? with what child of her own or child lost? And what had she covertly passed to Esme in her milk, what tastes, what feelings?

Not that Esme had done so well herself, her own milk running out after the first month. Well thank goodness for bottles and baby formula, she thought, pulling herself up. More reliable anyway, as the doctor had pointed out. At least you know the baby's getting enough. And that had tormented her, the thought of Suzanne starving without her being aware of it.

One evening when Suzanne was still a baby, watching her mix the formula and fill the bottle Aylene had commented, Mothering has become so scientific. And Esme was surprised by the note of regret. Did her mother actually feel she had missed something? She thought of the kampongs and markets of Penang, babies so easily held and nursed, sleeping in the folds of a sarong, or lugged on a big sister's hip. No prams, no bottles, no bassinets. But grandmothers, sisters, aunties all lending a hand. Who had mothered Aylene? Another ayah probably.

If she asked, would her mother do more than toss it aside: For heaven's sake, darling, what does it matter now?

—

Because what "doesn't matter," what we cut off from us by cognitive amputation, comes back to haunt us, i want to say for Esme — or is it to her standing there in the dim light of that 1940s kitchen, so much unsaid stifling in the air around her.

These assumptions the daily is grounded on, housed in. That you are "your mother's daughter" — the likeness that phrase insists on, insinuates: a replica.

And the likeness of lovers — have we assumed that too?

—

Later, when we went back to Penang, Whiteaways was one of those treats she reserved for me. At a glass-topped table in a room full of languid women sipping tea and chatting, i sat very straight on my wicker chair and was allowed to choose a millefeuille from the tiered plate the waiter patiently extended. She ordered iced coffee, her favourite, and smiled cautiously over its rim as i broke into the pastry with knife and fork.

Well? she would ask, is it scrumptious? And i was too young to hear the wistful echo of boarding school talk, the gloating reports of teashops other children with parents who visited would bring back to the dorm.

She asked what i liked best about the film we'd just seen, and so we would chat, like the others seated around us with their handbags and hats, their cigarettes curling enigmatic smoke. Having her all to myself, i wanted to keep her interest. Margo and Lucy were merely home with Amah and here she was, sitting expectantly in her floral print dress. That was her perfume i could smell in the sunjacket draped on the chair beside me.

Trying to sip, not gulp, my orange crush, i kept up a patter of invented talk while her eyes wandered over to other tables. A few women she knew, but only superficially. Mostly they were strangers. I didn't think to wonder where her friends were.

Walking back along Pitt Street, crowded and hot in the late afternoon, we shared a sense of elation despite the usual beggars, the usual throng of trishaw drivers soliciting us. She stopped suddenly at a carved entranceway and said, let's go in.

The Kuan Yin temple, blackened with years of incense, thick with smoke and the drone of men chanting. Did we take off our shoes? I don't remember. I only remember her holding my hand and whispering, we must be quiet now, afraid and impassioned at once, not mother, complicit, accomplice, as we ventured further into the strange-smelling dusk. Beyond an ornate pillar, a train of old men in saffron robes, heads shaved, palms folded together, the monotony of their voices rising like smoke.

There's Kuan Yin, she said. She sounded remote, as if she had gone somewhere. Where? i asked. Another man, not a monk, pushed by us with joss sticks burning. I felt uneasy. Are we supposed to be in here? SSh! Now she was angry. I didn't look at her face, i didn't see Kuan Yin, only the saffron men with hands folded, their quiet inturned look, the soft sound of their feet brushing the floor, oblivious.

—

Fragments of story. Telling them over, watching them revolve like magic lantern scenes in the dark that is about to become dawn. Every scene recalls another: endless cine footage of our childhood flickering in winter living rooms, wind-driven rain at the windows barely audible in that fascinated watching of our former selves. We chewed gum, spoke with Canadian accents, hummed rock 'n' roll, yet allowed ourselves to be ferried back on our parents' nostalgic comments — remember this? oh how could you forget that? — the almost-smell of coconut oil, of petrol fumes and dried fish tickling my nose . ...

I find no words for this threshold, though the sense of being suspended here is exquisite. Present in your absence, my love, loves echoing. It's still dark, the gulls are crying. Against the greying bowl of sky i can see their shapes swerve out over the lake and it gives me a sense of relief, of space. Below my window, the cat penetrates just-visible grass, alert to the tiniest waking movement of shrews. These are minutiae of a present that used to be *our* present, turning into another shell. Who are you out hunting your adolescence with? Retracing the subtlest of pathways on that old, loaded ground.

To avoid disappearing in guesswork coloured by fear, loss, i write my history here.

A book of mornings, morning that indistinct time (first light) when things have yet to harden into the clarity of the everyday, of separate categories, dissociated. At noon we pull in our senses, snails in the heat (poor overloaded antennae) and limit ourselves to what we select of the visible, the voluble, the sheer volume of the obvious.

Mourning the loss of early light which opens first to sound or smell or touch, not sight. The eye, unfocused, gazes at water, air, all that envelops us, pre-dates us. Post-dates us too. Mourning the loss of being before knowing narrowed into the dangerously exclusive we label meaningful, or what counts. "Knowing who your friends are." (Your lovers too?) And what about all that mothers, has mothered us into existence? Relations beyond number.

—

your whole body aches though it's your turn to stand watch. Banka Fever keeps running through your head, Banka Fever like a sign monotonously repeated. you hang onto it so your eyes will stay on the kerosene lamp the guards insist must be kept going. it keeps going all right, going in and out of focus. all your knobby bones ache, deep, deep through you. we're just loose bags of bone, P. had said. yet you must stand, it's your turn to do it.

stand up. open your eyes. what time is it? can you tell by the lamp? you open your eyes wider — the fuel level is almost where it was — you make yourself think beyond the lamp, beyond the whine of mosquitoes zooming in. sounds of restless turning just as incessant though you can't quite see who's awake. fevered moaning from the far corner. that must be the youngest of the Eurasian girls, the one whose sister worried about her refusing soup. don't scratch, you'll only make the bites worse. yesterday P. died, the day before it was N. the Aussie nurses are doing their best and they're up too. the least you can do is stay on your feet, don't think about those blasted mosquitoes. no blanket, no net — ha, forget all that. you try to pull your sleeves down — if you pull much further the cloth will rip. don't slump. if you slump the guard will be sure to appear and you'll get a jarring smack on the head. shift your weight, imagine you're a statue — Florence Nightingale? she didn't have to stand like this. but she was a nurse. what was it N. said about discovering what we're made of? we're made of nothing, we're made of fever and pain. well, listen then, to the creak of frogs in the swamp, someone pissing on the bamboo slats of the cesspool and walking back. you can't see stars though they must be out there. you can't hear the tramp of boots, but you can hear the Death Bird singing from the jungle. this is when people let go. this is when you hang on . . .

—

In mid-November there were revelations of a concentration camp in Holland. LIME PITS AND OVENS. The paper described how in one section of the camp a nursery was found, its walls decorated with scenes from Red Riding Hood and Babes in the Wood. A second section housed a mobile crematorium and two large ovens. It also housed a small air-tight cell in which ninety-four women had been locked for forty-eight hours.

Esme, who had picked up the paper with her morning groceries while Charles was sleeping off his late watch, felt compelled to recite the details over lunch. It says that one of the survivors of that cell became a raving lunatic — no wonder! How can they do such vile things? How can they decorate a nursery and torture innocent women at the same time?

Charles looked up from the loaf of bread he was slicing. Despite what your father thinks, war makes men less human not more so.

Human, she thought, what is human? It sounded like a foreign word. Glancing over at Suzanne she watched her trail a bread soldier through her soup with elaborate care, discovering how bread crumbles. That, she supposed, was natural curiosity, despite the mess it made. She stopped herself from rising to wipe off soupy fingers. What has happened to human beings? We, she had trouble thinking *we*, but Charles in his quiet way had touched on something, we aren't born evil, surely.

She began to have a recurring dream in which, herself a prisoner, she talked other prisoners into attempting an escape that only led them deeper into dungeons, hidden sluice-gates, frantic drowning. She woke appalled, tiptoed into her daughter's room and gazed at the small body abandoned, arms flung out, to sleep. Charles was still at work. The clock still ticked heavily on its stand in the hall. What kind of a world are we moving into?

In your condition, her father told her, you shouldn't be reading the papers at all.

What? And turn a blind eye? Pretend it isn't happening?

He took the barb but didn't respond. You need an evening off. Get Charles to take you out to a flick.

With a two-year-old on her hands, she was eight months pregnant in the heat of mid-summer, Christmas about to arrive. If she wasn't so tired, if Charles didn't have to work at night, they might see Joan Fontaine in *Jane Eyre* or Rita Hayworth in *Cover Girl*. They might slip into the streets of Casablanca with Humphrey Bogart and forget the rest.

Stifling the urge to let fly with all her stored-up criticism, she walked out of the room. At least, she thought, in his backhand way he does acknowledge that I work.

—

Curious about them, tiptoeing around the corner of the open doorway (don't bother Amah, stay away from the kitchen), drawn by her chuckle, the sound of their voices, companionable, pacing each other and their work, the sound of chopping, of water running, the clang of pots. Curious about what they ate when they weren't cooking for us, what they said to each other in Malay. Curious about Amah's teasing laughter, Eng Kim's blushes, the way she ducked her head at words we missed, or protested, or exclaimed, shocked. Amah told stories — that was clear — told wonderful stories that ended with laughter, always that deep throaty laugh rippling up from the heave of her baju. Amah's smile, wisps of hair escaping her bun, afloat like exclamation marks around her crinkly eyes, their liquid brown, her mobile mouth. What happened to your children, Amah? Always the same question. Always the same answer: dead, all dead — as she picked up the cleaver and made to chase us screaming into the garden.

We never asked Eng Kim because she was so clearly not much older than we were, though grave and austere at times. Eng Kim had a sense of what was proper and tried to impart it to us, gently, without much fuss, as if it were purely common sense and why couldn't we see that?

But Amah, Amah was a renegade, complicit and indulgent. Her Thai soul practised compassion salted with fun. When we languished in our rooms at the Mem's command (she was more Mem than Mummy then), when we brooded, supposedly remorseful for what we'd done, brooding in fact over our exile from the dinner table and all company, then Amah climbed the back stairs to slip us a bowl of congee or the remains of a meal, finger to her lips and a smile winking over the act as if it had not happened.

—

When the scene changes do the feelings change? Or do they get put away in a chest somewhere, for a rainy day? In Vancouver so much later, the Chinese figures carved in teak that Margo, Lucy and i polished so reluctantly every Saturday were as remote as Tuktoyaktuk. I made up stories about those venerable men in their longsleeved robes, those ladies smiling and strolling over a crescent moon of a bridge, the tea pavilion whose curving roof i squashed the corners of the polish rag against, trying to get out the dust. I didn't connect them with Eng Kim who never had time to stroll over a bridge, nor the crowded street in Georgetown where the furniture makers worked in a fragrance of camphorwood.

These had become the markers of someone else's life, a life i kept hidden away from my North Van friends who would find it odd, a curiosity shop, this houseful of Chinese furniture and parents who spoke with what then seemed exaggerated politeness — another world of manners, of phrases. A world i left behind to belong in the new one.

What i left behind is not left so much as embalmed in my childhood. Like a ghost it goes on living alongside this reality, occasionally felt, an inner twinge, the merest flicker of memory, unlocatable, indistinct. There are no words for these almost-recognitions, because they are not memories dressed in the detail of half-fictionalized scenes. They hover beyond our attempts to resurrect them along the coordinates of this time, this present person. Who could never have been imagined in that other reality.

Just as the reality of war fades. Teacher strikes, declining retail profits take precedence in the news. The ordinary preoccupations of the daily. As if it were a relief to stop thinking about the larger implications of what we are involved in. So in your less and less frequent calls i avoid asking what you plan to do, or worse, when you might come home.

Home . . . that abyss after a word. What the musing words have been trying to keep at bay: dread, the peculiar dread of the about-to-be — tearing loss, disappearance. Lori, i know the signs. You are about to step out of my life and into my world of ghosts. No matter how i try to bring you close, your body is already fading from mine. That's what hurts most, the insult to how immediately present we were for each other.

Insult? you ask pointedly, it's your world of ghosts you're talking about, not mine. So i carry on, as i carry on all our conversations in my head. Not *memento*, not even *evidence*: those words won't do. It's the horror of knowing that, even as i remember in bits and pieces, i alter you into the ghost of someone you weren't.

—

You must have been a beautiful baby, coz baby, look at you now. Black and white snapshots of two tykes, war babies with flamboyant cheeks on a plaid blanket, the oldest in a halo of curls clasping the baby lying huge on short legs stuck out before her. Winter coats and leggings. Radiant smiles, one of proud possession, the other of trusting contentment. Posed there for the camera that would inscribe the moment for grandparents and aunties, for future reminiscence in unforeseen locales.

By April of that year, the last year, as it turned out, of the war, the Allies were riding an incoming tide. In Germany, the Americans were continuing their drive across the country — Trier and Cologne were already liberated. The Russians had discovered Auschwitz and were advancing on Berlin. In the Pacific, the long struggle for Iwo Jima, only 750 miles from Yokohama, was over, giving the U.S. a new air base. Optimism pervaded the autumn streets of Melbourne, hawked by newsboys, dispensed by radio commentators, illustrated over and over again in the newsreels that preceded every movie.

In St. Kilda and off the record, Esme worried about this new baby, so unlike her firstborn, who gazed at the world with grave eyes. *Jeepers, creepers, where'd you get those weepers?* Or was it *peepers?* Fair-haired and fair-skinned, this child watched her mercurial older sister with caution. Esme had already caught Suzanne trying to poke the baby's eyes out with the tip of an umbrella. Queuing up at the greengrocer's, the butcher's, she peered uneasily through the window at the pram, Suzanne in reins tied to the handlebar and supposedly standing guard.

Aylene decided that her oldest granddaughter felt neglected and spent hours making a mammoth teddy bear out of real Australian fleece. Viktor advised checking her bowels and dosing her with Eno's. No conflict this time over a name for the baby: Margo, they all agreed, suited a serious child.

—

I don't know which is more exasperating, Esme tried to make light of it, my parents or my children.

You make life at the office seem positively simple, Dorothy agreed. They were sitting in her flat on one of Esme's rarer and rarer visits. As usual, Dorothy's lounge, though small, was tastefully arranged. Nothing seemed out of its habitual place. She had even managed to afford a Chinese table displaying at least two magazines Esme wished she had time to read.

On her way over, Esme reminded herself not to rattle on about the children for fear of touching a raw spot. There was still no word of Brian and they barely mentioned his name now. They never mentioned Peggy. But then Dorothy *was* Suzanne's godmother. It might be good for her to get involved. Besides, what else was there to talk about?

Quite honestly, I'm at my wit's end. I can't leave them alone for an instant.

Who, my dear? It was moments like this when Dorothy seemed to disappear that Esme dreaded. A sudden void in their conversation, at the edge of which images of emaciated POWs hovered.

She covered it over with a laugh. The children of course. We thought Suzanne would be delighted to have a baby sister. Any normal child would, don't you think?

Ah well, I don't know much about children — Dorothy was shifting the ice in her glass — but then we were both children once, normal or not. (Now she was back.) How did *you* feel, for instance, when your brother was born?

Oh I loved him, Esme promptly said. It was such a relief to have someone smaller.

Relief? Rattling back on the tram alone — Aylene was in charge and she felt unaccountably free — she wondered why she had said it. She had barely known him, stuck, as they were, in separate boarding schools. Dorothy had gone on to ask about her mother in those early days before school. I don't remember, Esme said. She was a goddess, beautiful, remote, completely absorbed in my father's world. I think I never knew whether she'd be pleased to see me or upset at how I looked.

Did smaller mean someone she could torment — she hadn't tormented Will, had she? Smaller meant a companion in misery. That's a pretty grim picture of childhood, she thought. Suzanne couldn't possibly feel that way, not with doting parents and grandparents on every side.

But that was her own picture of her daughter, she revised, staring at the rain-streaked glass lit up in passing flashes by the shop signs outside, dark to light to dark again. How could one determine what was in the glass and what was behind it?

Here on the tram she was glad to be alone for once. Glad to have Aylene willing to play mother, yes, even with the friction. She couldn't have managed these last few years without her. There was still a torn edge somewhere that Aylene tried to cover over, glue together in fact. But all those certainties about her mother's complete lack of parenting were beginning to fade. What was a good mother? Perhaps it was essential to ask a different question, to ask how does one manage, after all, to remain a person?

—

There is darkness in our bedroom window i keep gazing at, as if my focus could be anaesthetized there, away from your voice coming between long gaps where silence vibrates. As if i could shift the focus from each pulsebeat the silence is occupied by. Preoccupied. With a long line of nothing connecting us half a continent apart. Have you really called just to say your mother is better, the weather is terrible in Iowa?

I tell you the willows by the lake are turning yellow, the grass is growing wildly. There are even violets, fragrant and tiny at the edge of the lawn. Your famous spring, you say. And silence rides in again.

All right, i'll risk it. So when are you coming back?

More silence. A quickening in the window, a darker shape in the darkness perhaps. I've been meaning to tell you . . . i think you already know . . . What phrases are you turning over?

There's no way to say this . . . (of course) . . . I've thought about it a lot while i've been here. I need to live on my own.

The words, although foreseen, open like a chasm in the floor. Silence my silence now, choked. Then one word burning through the images that flicker in the time it takes not to say it — why? why? We were holding hands at the ferry when you left, we turned toward each other's opening body, your face shining I love you in the stillness of the rain. And a cold voice takes over, perfectly rational. There is someone else?

A pause. You're taken aback, you thought i didn't know. Reluctantly your words trickle out. There is, Suzanne, but that's not really the reason.

What is the reason then? My voice is automatic, a cover for the pain i set in the window with the shape that keeps shifting beyond recognition. Still i can hear it myself, the parental tone you're quick to evade.

Perhaps we'd better talk about this later.

Don't hang up now, you can't hang up. I need to know . . . What went wrong? i ask. Like a child, i think to myself as you say it:

Don't sound so innocent. You've got your part in all this too.

The shape, it's a cedar branch in the wind, is coming clearer. Light shifting its overlapping fronds. Scales of the old familiar. The hide and seek we keep playing in the old roles.

We just don't live in the same reality — your way of erasing our ghost-written bond. Its unfinished stories playing through us.

—

After the war was over and before her parents returned to England, Viktor filled out a memo book in his crabbed medical hand, a book of home remedies for Esme to take with her to Penang in case doctors, at least English ones, were hard to find in all that post-war chaos. Remedies (recipes, with proportions specified) for different kinds of catarrh — bronchial, both acute and chronic, nasal, ophthalmic, pharyngeal (plain old sore throat). Remedies for ear ache, insect bite, Singapore foot, even indigestion. Ingredients, some abbreviated and difficult to decipher, included substances like tannic acid, nux vomica, methyl salicylate, ammonium carbonate — did she bring these with her on the ship from Melbourne? He tried to cover every eventuality. There was even a recipe for *Lotus amygdalae Composita* (*a good hand & face lotion*).

So she gathered her own dispensary, kept in a padlocked cupboard with air vents on the breezeway just outside the kitchen. Out of this box, with its mysterious medicinal smell, she treated all emergencies. Amah's fever, Eng Kim's burns, Ungimah's bruises from her husband's drunken rages. Every morning Margo, Lucy and i lined up for a spoonful of cod liver oil.

Every few months we were ordered to appear with the dog behind us, each receiving the worm pill like a wafer on our tongues. (When the dog, "you bad boy," spat his out, she covered his muzzle so he was forced to swallow.)

It's a good thing you're a doctor's daughter. Her father underwrote his handing-on of knowledge. After all, she would be responsible for an entire household in the tropics.

Nursing approved finally as part of Mem Sahib-hood.

—

I am sitting with my sisters on the edge of a low wall that encloses the fountain and the toddler's wading pool. Sitting very cocky, legs apart, one arm braced against my thigh, while Margo and Lucy perch diminutively on either side, their knees up, Lucy's hair plastered to her face. We sit in our bathing costumes, baggy in front, wrinkly on the side, and the tropical heat bleaches the sky white behind us. This is the Penang Swimming Club and the sea, that milky sea with its ikan sembilan and jellyfish, rolls away toward a hazy mainland horizon.

Immediately behind us stands Dorothy in pearl necklace and jet-black costume — she hasn't been swimming yet, won't perhaps, will sit with Mummy in the atap-roofed kiosk where drinks are served, sip a g-and-t and chat. For now she is standing in the shallow pool with one hand on Margo's shoulder and the other on her hip, her curled hair swept to the side Lana Turner fashion. Over a radiant smile she raises one eyebrow slightly — Mummy, peering into the Rollei, has just suggested that we look like street urchins. I hope you don't mean me, my dear!

I am enjoying the wet and the smiles and the fun. Earlier, when Syce opened the door of the black car, i watched slender legs emerge, and then the rest of a Dorothy i almost remembered, Dorothy brought from the ferry in a whirl of bright chatter, perfume, and gifts — all the goodnesses, the how you've growns, so this is Lucy, Amah holding Lucy's reluctant hand. Dorothy who worked for Planned Parenthood now. Dorothy the career woman, Mummy said.

Staring into the photos from that visit, i try to make out a Melbourne shadow around her eyes, a slightly drawn line between her brows. Her face resists, sunny and clear of grief.

By the afternoon i have claimed her. Allowed to swim on my own in the adults' pool, i hang around the children's one, eavesdropping as they sit with an eye on the little ones, laughing, commenting, touching one another lightly on the arm. My mother has become girlish and this glimpse of her is fascinating. I want them to notice me, include me in the warmth that radiates between them. I also want to be invisible, so i can hear things i'm not supposed to. And i keep an eye on Margo and Lucy, in case they forget — they could so easily forget about all three of us.

Later, my sisters towelled and busy on the sand with buckets, i get tired of showing off splashy jumps to no one, so i walk into the kiosk and catch the disappearing tail of something, bad hats and communist guerillas — you wouldn't believe it, he has to carry a revolver with him.

Well, she encircles my waist, has the diver come up with any pearls yet?

Their wicker chairs, the bracelet sliding down her arm, their tall sweating drinks, all of it hovers, ghostly in any re-creation. A larger history was sitting where they sat, turning a present already slipping from them. And though the tile and concrete

of that pool was still imprinted on the soles of my feet, it too
was sliding into legend, to be repeated and then eclipsed, like
the story of Brian, like the story of Peggy.

—

. . . Muntok . . . Banka Fever . . . a wavering path into the jungle
. . . the living weak digging graves with makeshift tools . . . no
markers, nothing left

> *Each in a burial space,*
> *By women's hands, filled in and beautified*
>
> *. . . a cross of twigs so simply tied . . .*

—

Wispy and silhouette-clear as a cedar plume drawing unreadable characters in the wind against that grey, that light nothing-
ness, something keeps inventing itself. There was always something and nothing, it just wasn't clear how they turn in the wind.
How they might even be the same.

I hang onto that slight thread in the darkness of you gone. A
nameless space (pre)occupied by names.

And all my stories turn in this transition hour just before dawn,
when light begins to intimate the differences between things

still rooted deep in earth's shadow. I think of you in the Midwest where it has been light for some time and the furrows are drawing you out beyond town. You return to your own layers of family never and, yes, ever outgrown. The snapshots we take and are taken by. The photos you dreamed of finally cutting up.

I imagine your feet stepping out, one after the other. I can't begin to imagine your feet or what you are feeling there now. In coastal shadow two hours behind, in the shadow of our coming undone i see almost nothing with extra clarity. How we avoided speaking of that earlier war which drove you out of the Midwest to Canada, thinking to escape complicity.

We *are* complicit, yes. Folded into the wreckage of grief and power.

Light is beginning to flare behind the leaves, to glisten and lean in along the limbs of those water trees that stand, seem always to have stood, just at the edge of our window frame. Soon long cottony filaments will launch on a breeze spinning them into nests, the gullets of fish, sludgy eaves troughs we failed to clean, an unseasonal snow no camera will catch.

I pull your sleeve. They go on spinning out of eyeshot, snapshot, beyond the reach of evidence. The stories we invent and refuse to invent ourselves by, all unfinished . . .

ACKNOWLEDGEMENTS

The personages in *Taken* are characters, fictionalized beyond the ordinary fictionalizing "memories" assume. They do, however, have their roots in family stories as well as documentary, especially the painful testimony of survivors of Japanese prisoner-of-war camps in Singapore and Indonesia. For source material, my gratitude to the following:

My mother, Edrys Buckle; my father and stepmother, Arthur and Anne Buckle; my sister, Pam Pedersen; my uncle, Keith Lupprian; Jean and Nick Waddell; Lavinia Warner and John Sandilands, *Women Beyond the Wire* (particularly for the quoted lines on page 129); Agnes Newton Keith, *Three Came Home*; Tim Bowden, *Changi Photographer: George Aspinall's Record of Captivity*; Ken Attiwill, *The Singapore Story*; Noel Barber, *Sinister Twilight*; *The Sydney Morning Herald* (1942); *The Age* (Melbourne, 1944); *The Vancouver Sun* (1991). Thanks to Phyllis Webb and Coach House Press for permission to quote from *Water and Light* (epigraph). Thanks also to Cheryl Carter for great assistance with initial research and to the Ruth Wynn Woodward Chair, Women's Studies, Simon Fraser University, for funding that assistance.

I wish to most particularly thank my original editor, Stan Dragland, for his careful reading of the manuscript, invaluable prompting, and wise suggestions, and Martha Sharpe, my editor at House of Anansi Press, for attentive advice. My thanks also go to other manuscript readers who gave me greatly appreciated critical response: Jam Ismail, Leila Sujir, Ellen Seligman, Kathy Mezei, Bridget MacKenzie, and, in early stages of writing, Betsy and Steven Warland. Thanks also to Cheryl Sourkes and Lydia Kwa for insightful discussion.

Grateful appreciation to Bridget MacKenzie for her constant encouragement, and to Julian Isett for rescuing me at all hours of the day from computer crises. Above all, heart-felt gratitude to Zasep Tulku Rinpoche who counsels always compassionate view.

For financial support, my thanks to B.C. Cultural Services for a short-term grant, 1991.

Parts of this novel have appeared in *The Capilano Review* and *West Coast Line*.